Honey
on the
Moon

Honey
on the
Moon

MAUDE HUTCHINS

William Morrow & Company
New York 1964

THERE'S HONEY ON THE MOON TONIGHT
(*as often sung by* Fats Waller)

Words by Haven Gillespie *and* Mack Davis.
Music by J. Fred Coots

There's honey on the moon tonight—
It's a sin if we waste it.

Come along and let's taste it—
Had it ordered for you.

There's honey on the moon tonight.
Tho' a little off season—
It is there for a reason—
For a dream to come true.

251192

Honey
on the
Moon

1

Three weeks ago today I was married. This is my honeymoon. I can hardly believe it. My husband, what a strange word it is to me still: *husband;* my dictionary is at my elbow but I am too lackadaisical to look up what it means—to *husband,* I suppose, as if I were the grain. My dog, from whom I have been separated for three weeks, is staring at me. She lies across the threshold, her nose between her paws, just staring. Her dear soft brown eyes are questioning and a little anxious.

"Sydney dearest, I am quite all right, you needn't worry," I say to her and her tail moves twice from left to right over the carpet without enthusiasm.

In the little book I am writing in, my childhood consists of fifty pages and I thumb back over them looking for a clew, a reason, for me; but the notations

are formal and very discreet, the handwriting as
pinched as my little nose used to feel on a cold day
in the country. Yes here is something: "Allyn made
me stick out my tongue and he put his skate on it.
It was awful. I couldn't take it [my tongue] away.
The beast." Yes I remember, tears came into my eyes
but even through the foggy bluish blur I saw, as if
underwater in the pond, the sadistic grin of the little
monster, the grin of the master.

Well, didn't Derek only yesterday, my darling
Derek, indulge in some boyish cruelty to gain my
emotional attention, and he is twenty years older
than me, and thirty years older than Allyn was that
winter afternoon by the edge of the pond.

What else? . . . How silly! It might as well be in
code. What does "Coconut" mean, for instance, followed by a lot of exclamation marks?

Let's see . . . "Allyn showed me something today."
I blush, my face is suffused, I have forgotten . . . I
don't remember; what was it Allyn showed me? No
hint is given in my little girl's diary but I see on my
wedding night Derek standing by my bed. "Don't
be afraid, Sigourney," he said in a muffled voice,
"look at me," but I looked steadfastly into his eyes,
brown eyes, the color of the banisters but with a
blue flame in them like a sulphurous match. "Sigourney look at me." "I am," I said, "I will," and I

closed my eyes so tight that a golden sun seemed to
rise over a black horizon and splinter into pieces of
violet fire.

"May I look at you?" he said gently.

"No," I sobbed.

"A fine thing," I heard him say, and he flung up
the shade with a snap and the tassle jumped up and
down. I opened my eyes just enough to see him
through my lashes, profiled against the window that
made him look as if he were painted on glass, a primitive naked Adam.

He turned toward me again. "Do you mind if I
smoke?" he said coolly.

I couldn't help smiling, I almost giggled, I did
giggle, "Where are your *pockets?*" I snickered,
"Where do you keep your cigarettes?" I choked,
"And—and—your lighter I gave you for Christmas
with—with your *initials* on it?" I was a little hysterical, I suppose, but I still think it was funny.
Derek didn't at all. He sat down in a chintz-covered
chair with big blue roses on it and lit his cigarette.
The flash from his lighter illumined the handsome
face, the straight nose with thin nostrils that flared
a little when he breathed, the arching brows neat as
a woman's, and the smooth dark warm cheeks. A dear
face as beautiful as if Raphael painted it. I felt soft
and womanly and kind and pretty.

"Please put on your clothes," I said timidly.

"Are we going somewhere?" he said frostily.

"I like you in your clothes," I said.

He stood up and put out his cigarette in an ash tray, brutally, as if he was stomping something to death. The flame in his eyes leaped up.

"Do I look funny?" he said, "terribly funny? Do I look like an ape? What is so funny?"

"I'm not laughing," I said. "I wasn't laughing at *you*, I was laughing at something else."

I lay on my back with a pink sheet up under my chin, I looked straight into his eyes as I love to do, as I had been doing for a whole year, the year of our engagement, the year that was supposed to make me come to my senses.

He reached out and looped his silk dressing gown off the post of his bed as if it were a halyard off a mast and turning his back, tied it around his waist. He sat down on my bed and returned my steady gaze. . . .

"Sigourney," he said finally.

"Derek?"

"*Do* you love me?"

"Oh yes, my darling Derek, I do," I said whole-heartedly. And I reached my bare arms up and out toward him. I took him around the neck. It felt like a smooth Doric column. As deftly as he had slipped his gown off the post, he lowered his head and whisked off the pink sheet, and it billowed like a spinnaker for a second and fell to the floor in an airless heap. I was amazed at his sleight of hand, deft and quick and articulated as I knew him to be and light on his feet, graceful as a hawk over a field, as a gull over an inlet.

"Derek," I screeched and I covered my breasts with the span of my left hand and my private self with my right. I lowered my chin and saw my navel exposed like a bite in a peach, but there was nothing more I could do. I immediately regretted my girlish modesty and tried to forget the ridiculous screech. I felt ashamed, not of my nudity but of my modesty, which seemed silly. But as I let go of myself and again encircled Derek's warm neck, I pulled his head down so that he could not see my nakedness, I felt his nose between my breasts, he disengaged himself easily and straightening up, he looked me over from chin to toe, grazing me with half-closed eyes. As they wandered over me, I felt their spark in specific places and my body responded as if he traced a nimble finger, his almond-shaped nails indenting me. The network of his gaze marked an intricate design of pleasure along my skin. He did indeed spin a web with his eyes, it was as if he knew how and had done it before, an educated spider with something definite

in mind. I did not struggle against the sweet and ten-
uous incarceration and I felt like an exhausted and
frangible prisoner who might at last rest. It wasn't
my fault any longer. He slid his forefinger down the
opening of the slippery silk dressing gown and
spreading it wide, hovered over me. He so gently
let himself down as if I were asleep and he did not
want to awaken me. His mouth came down on mine
that was open and it tasted like vanilla, was it the
memory of the sweet white wine, the Chablis, we
had had for dinner, or was it the éclair he bought
me for dessert? As he closed in on me, I arched my
back, nobody having told me to do so, and separated
my legs. But at the contact of his skin, as his whole
weight descended on me, as he let go of my mouth
and I felt his hot breath in the hollow of my neck
and one hand as if he were a dying man clenching
a fistful of my cool flesh behind, I cried "No!" in a
clarion voice like the Angel Gabriel.

The clock in the square rang out clear and sten-
torian as if I had signaled to it. Midnight, it sang
and the length of time of that number was the pause
that Derek, straightening a little, waited. But he had
reduced his weight and I breathed easily again.

"Good morning," he said, and he raised himself
and returned to the chair with the blue roses on it,
stretching out his long legs and lifting his chin.

"Where," he said finally, "do you want me to sleep?"

"Why here, Derek, beside me," I said. "Please don't be angry, please love me, Derek."

"Christ," he said.

"Derek, let me do it," I said in a low voice, what did I mean? and he said "What?" in a startled voice.

"Please," I said, "please put out that light over there and come back."

"For Christ's sake, Sigourney, I am a man . . ."

"I know it, Derek."

"If I didn't know you so well I would think you were a nasty little flirt." No that isn't what he said, it was worse than that.

"Derek!" I wailed.

"I'm not one of your twenty-year-old boy friends," he said crossly. "Don't play with me, I need a grown woman . . ."

"Ah," I said, "but it was me, it was me I thought you loved."

"Oh Sigourney, shut up."

"But isn't it?"

"Yes, stop it."

"What are the grown women you have loved like?" I said.

"Look Sigourney, let's cut this out, I am exhausted." He snapped out the light and I saw him coming toward the bed like a silhouette, his shadow dropped over me. Again I feel like a small animal, a hare in the shadow of a hawk.

"Please put on your pyjamas," I said plaintively.

What a patient man, I don't know why he didn't strangle me.

"Yes Sigourney," he said, "forget it . . ."

"Pleasant dreams," he said as he got in beside me. "Goodnight little Sigourney," and he kissed my cheek. In no time at all he was asleep.

I was amazed. "Why, he is asleep," I said out loud, and nothing is solved, nothing at all. I lay with my eyes wide open without stirring. I heard the clock sing out one, two, and three. *There's Honey on the Moon Tonight. . . . Come along and let's taste it . . .*

"Derek," I whispered. No answer. I moved close to him and lay my cheek against his neck. Did the pulse there quicken? No it was my own. I lifted my thigh and placed it over his. I put my fist into his diagonal armpit and he did not move. I timed my breathing to his and caressed him under his pyjamas, his skin was as smooth as mine, his chest hard like a cardboard box and it rose and fell under my hand. My heart began to beat fast and irregularly, it was as if I were stealing something out of a cupboard. I ran my palm the length of his leg, I cupped it and felt his interwoven muscles, I brought it back up the inside of his thigh and it was soft and satin fine there

as a woman. My cheeks felt on fire as I took him in
my fist and wrapped my legs around his quiescent
thigh. I was quite mad, I felt a cold froth on my lips
and I licked it off with my tongue. I felt a rhythmic
and frenzied desire for the sleeping man. "Derek,"
I cried and my voice sounded strange and frantic
like a child lost in the woods. With a sinuous move-
ment, not too sudden, smooth as silk, he turned toward me and it was I, my hands, my fist, that guided
him as if he were a blind man and he was, he did
not open his eyes. I felt his heart and heard it like
a hammer in my temples, his blood sang in my ears,
I lost my balance, I forgot the parts of my body, I
thought for a moment he was between my breasts
and I longed for more as it all slid away from me,
out of my mind, out of my body. Good-by, I wept,
good-by, it is over.

"How awful, it is finished," I sobbed. "Derek,
Derek, how sad it is over."

"Sigourney, Sigourney, hush, be quiet . . ."

He held me close and kissed my eyelids. "Go to
sleep," he said.

"I can't," I said, "I can't," and I did. I slept like
a cat, my toes twitching, my eyelids shivering.

Ah Sydney, why do you stare so?

2

I awoke slowly next morning only four hours after I had gone to sleep. I had dreamed absolutely nothing and I felt quite safe, I was covered with a brand new quilt to the chin and it smelled like cucumbers. I remembered nothing until I heard unfamiliar sounds in the street where there should have been fields— the low off-key whistle of the hired man with his wheelbarrow, Jenny the mare stomping in her stall and the swallows in the ivy. I sat straight up and the slinky quilt fell away from my naked torso (Where are my cozy red pyjamas?), the door that had a porcelain knob with pink roses on it opened, a foot had given it a quick shove, and Derek, my fiancé, stood there with a tray in both hands. The burnt smell of coffee, I always have tea, came in with him. He was fully dressed and he stood straight and lean and handsome.

"Derek!" I cried and I pulled up the quilt with one hand and pushed my hair out of my eyes with the other.

"Who else," he said.

"I'm married!" I sang out, it was unbelievable. There stood my husband.

"You certainly are," he said seriously, "and so am I."

As he set the tray on my knees, I noticed the delicate convolutions of his ear and the short hairs on his neck, the flaring nostril, and a return of last night's desire hard and insistent almost made me cry out. I gave a quivering sigh and lifted my cup of coffee with two hands but still the fragile cup danced in its saucer and the spoon spun off onto the tray.

Derek picked it up. "Take it easy, little one," he said and he smiled at me, an even friendly smile. I looked at him, I tried to tell him, but how does a woman let a man know? He stooped and kissed me and his lips were cool, but the smell of my own perfume on him set my ears ringing.

"You smell like me," I muttered, and lowered my eyes in confusion.

"I thought I washed it off," he said tactlessly and he rubbed at his neck hard. "Do I really?"

"Don't you like it?" I said, I was near tears. Conscious of my nakedness beneath the quilt, I longed for him to take me in his arms. I wanted to feel him under the roughness of his brown wool suit that I remembered so well in the country. I wanted to feel the slight bend of his knee between my legs as I listened for the sound of my father's footsteps.

"Please get me my nightie," I said chokingly, "or something."

"Righto," he said and he pulled it out of my shiny new overnight bag like a long lacy stocking without disturbing anything else. He is amazing. I wondered how I was going to get it on but I needn't have. As discreet as a well-trained waiter at the Waldorf, he picked up the tray and left the room. The door closed after him noiselessly. I was taken aback. I wondered. I looked at my beautiful trousseau nightgown, diaphanous and fawn-colored, the same tone as my skin, that I had taken half a day to choose at the shop, and the aging girl over the counter with elongated mascaraed eyes and blue shadow put on up to her plucked eyebrows had said, "My dear he'll love it, you couldn't have chosen better," and I had felt offended at my open secret, the secret that was no secret, that on the following Tuesday I would go to bed with Derek in a fawn-colored nightgown you could see through. I had thought of shaving myself as I had my armpits but I didn't know and there was certainly no one to ask. I thought of buying a diaper-shaped panty to wear underneath, but even then my navel would show like a violet hole. Well, I hadn't dared put it on at all but had sneaked into bed with nothing on and pulled the pink sheet up to my chin and waited.

Last night comes back to me in detail and in technicolor. How stupid and idiotic I must have seemed to Derek, a man of the world and forty years old. The memory of the almost painful pleasure that came to me in the dark night makes my head ache.

I slipped on the wisp of a nightie and tiptoed over the soft carpet to the mirror. I had scarlet polish on my toenails for the first time in my life and I admired my pretty narrow feet with five red candy-like shells on each. The nagging desire went away and a euphoria, the kind that follows physical fatigue, came over me. An electrical discharge in the stuff of the gown made it cling in parts to my skin and I plucked it away and looked at myself. Could it be Sigourney, that girl reflected there, Sigourney who had never worn anything but boy's pyjamas before and mismated socks to keep her cold toes warm? I saw a very slim, it is true, girl's body, but it was nicely rounded over the hips and the thighs were curved, the knees small with perceptibly full calves and very slight ankles like an antelope's. The breasts were the prettiest, round as two apples with pink tips the color of strawberry jam, the only color anywhere, not

counting the amber shade of my skin which is really
no color at all, as atmospheric as the beautiful
nightie that didn't hide a thing, it was like a breath,
that's all. At last I stared at the place that confounded
me, the place that got the better of me, that would
not hide. It looked like a tuft of moss. I sighed, and
turning, looked over my shoulder and was startled
at the nakedness, the blinding nakedness, of my
rounded behind in the broad daylight of the room,
cut right in two as it was, drawn as if with a black
pencil smack in the middle by a lovesick artist. I
looked back with relief at the comparative modesty
of the front of me. The tuft of moss was like a chestnut burr, denser but the same color as the hair hanging over my forehead, the same warm shade. I
blushed, I could not help it, but no blood ever shows
in my cheeks; the blush did not reflect in the mirror.
I looked under my arms and thought they looked a
little indecent, shaved like that and bald—for whom?

What was I supposed to do now? Where was
Derek? I pulled up the transparent nightie not to
slip on it and got back in bed.

"Derek," I called. There was no answer.

"Derek?"

I leaped out of bed thinking I was safe in my
pyjamas and enveloped in the amber cloud tore into
the tiny kitchenette. No Derek; the dishes had been

washed and put away, everything shone, brand new.
A note conspicuously pinned against the door said,
Sigourney, read me. With a funny unexplained sub-
jectless fear I read it. *Sweetheart I've gone for a walk.
Back soon. Derek.* What! Had I thought that he was
gone forever? Possibly.

"But do bridegrooms go for walks on their honeymoons?" I asked out loud. I shrugged, quite at a loss.

I washed in the little cubicle of a bathroom where
the shower curtain was still soaking wet from Derek's
ablutions and a single thumbprint of his indented the
toothpaste tube. I smiled with pleasure at this new
intimacy and nodded at myself in the mirror over
the basin, You are a married woman now. It's nice
isn't it.

I dressed in the sleek skirt of my going-away suit
that was so elegant and expensive, and a fresh white
blouse with rhinestone buttons. I twisted the plain
gold wedding ring on my finger and stared into the
bluish white light of the big solitaire diamond that
Derek had given me when we became engaged. As I
drew on my long sheer stockings and slid the blue
garters over my toes and ankles, I remembered the
colored maid, Elizabeth, who had put them on for
my wedding. Cook was jealous and stood in the door-
way in a dirty apron with a sneer on her wide Irish
face. "Miss doesn't like fussing over," she said, "leave

her be." I had overheard my mother a week before talking to Daddy who wasn't listening. "Paul I want Sigourney to have a little maid to dress her, to put on her stockings, I'll pay for it myself, my little maid always dressed me and Sigourney should have a little maid to put on her stockings just this once." Her soft wheedling voice died away. . . . "My little Sigourney must have a little maid to put on her stockings just this once," she said. Dear Daddy must have agreed because a colored girl from the village showed up in a black dress and a short black apron just like a real personal maid and I was rather pleased. I did not show my embarrassment and tried to act as if I were used to it. She slid the stockings up my long bare legs and gazed at me admiringly. "My but you're pretty, missy." She gave a great sigh. "I guess maybe *he* gonna take dese loby stockins *off.*" She rolled her eyes like marbles in a puzzle, the blood rushed to my face almost blinding me but I knew my cheeks were as pale as a lady's, only my lips trembled. "Don be scared," she whispered. "You gonna *like* it, and he lucky man to git you, all fresh like a daisy, my oh my!"

I put on my high-heeled patent leather pumps and wandered teeteringly over the little apartment. I have never cared much for my surroundings, indoors, I mean, and I rather love worn old rugs, indetermi-

nate colors, slits in the shades and even disorder, the
way it was at home, but this little place I look over
with pleasure, it is like a doll's house; Derek and his
sister Louise did it and Derek's mother paid for it for
a year as a wedding present. A year, I think, a whole
year with Derek, and an uneasiness comes over me,
my throat aches. *Where is he?* I am lonely.

The telephone rang. Even it sounded new, almost
false, like on the stage. And as I haven't rehearsed
my act I don't know just where it is.

"Hello?"

"Peter?"

"No."

"I must have the wrong number," said a strange
voice crossly and she hung up.

I feel even lonelier, I am almost frightened. Why
I don't *even* know my own address or my telephone
number, my own name is brand new, Mrs. Derek
Wagstaff, suppose I should forget it! What has become of Sigourney Logan? I pick up the telephone
again, I'll call Daddy, he'll come and get me.

"Hello?"

"Delia, this is Sigourney. Is Daddy there?"

"Oh Miss Sigourney, the mister's gone to the post
office and your mama is still asleep. Is something
wrong? Are you sick, child?"

"Oh no, Delia, I—I . . ." What a little fool I was.

What was there to say? "Never mind, Delia, don't say I called, I just forgot something."

"I guess you lost something you never going to find, miss, Saints preserve us," and Delia snorted, I imagined her wide grin and bleary eye.

"Good-by, Delia," I said haughtily.

"Good-by, miss, Mrs. Wagstaff," Delia corrected herself.

I heard a scraping and a thumping in the hall and another bell rang, short and rude, my nerves jumped. The kitchen door flew open.

"Expressman!"

"Oh hello," I said sheepishly, for a moment I had thought it would be Mac, the dear brown expressman at home who used to toss me in the air and called me Sigourney Junior.

"Mrs. Wagstaff here?"

I looked behind me.

"Your mother home?"

"Oh," I felt the painful blush that never betrayed me. "I am Mrs. Wagstaff," I said, looking beyond him, "and that's my trunk." A young lad stood there, too, his cap in his hands, staring at me, taking me in, admiring me.

"Hi," I said gratefully, he was my age, a country boy.

"Yes ma'am," he said and the two of them end-over-ended the trunk into the kitchen. "Okay?" said the big man and he handed me a dirty pencil and a slip of paper. "Sign here." Cheerfully I wrote *Sigourney* and anxiously, *Wagstaff*. I could feel him watching me, I felt his eyes on my ankles and on my waist, at the same time I knew the boy was gazing around the little place at the shiny sink, the stainless steel, and into the living room at the silky curtains, the rosy carpet. I handed back the slip and the pencil.

"The Giants beat the Mets," said the boy and he flushed.

"Bye now," said the big man, incongruously, I thought. Mac would have said "Good day, ma'am" to a married woman.

Had I been too friendly? "Thank you," I said. "Please close the door as you go out."

Poor Daddy spent a lot of money on that trunk, I said to myself as I examined it, its heavy brass hinges and corners and the sturdy lock, and a big deep scratch on it already. Giants? Are there really giants here? There could be. I can't open the trunk, Derek has the key. I began to count the glasses in the cupboard, there were so many, a dozen of everything, pretty glasses on long stems, thin and dangerous. I handled them gingerly. The ones at home were big and solid, a handful, even the sherry glasses were sturdy. They had nicks in them ever since I

could remember. Delia was clumsy, what a racket
she made in the pantry over the dishes. Mother used
to shake her head and smile wearily as if it were no
use but Daddy didn't hear anything unusual. An
electric clock hummed on the wall, I watched the
scarlet second hand go round smoothly, the icebox
shut itself off and I opened the door, it turned right
on again. It was stacked so neatly it looked as if
everything in it were made of plastic, there were no
little chipped bowls with delicious leftovers in them,
I shut the door quickly to save electricity.

I sat on the little three-legged high stool that was
set conveniently by the sink and looked out the single
window that had a pink ruffled curtain framing it
like a valentine and saw a square of sky. The sun had
suddenly gone round a corner and it was almost dark
in the kitchen.

"Oh dear what can the matter be," I sang. *"Three
old ladies got stuck in the lavat'ry, They were there
from Monday till Saturday, Nobody knew they were
there . . ."*

The telephone rang again and I made a dash for
it, it might be Derek.

"Hello?"

"Peter?" said a man's voice.

"No," I said and I laughed.

"Wrong number," said the voice, a pleasant sonorous voice, "sorry."

"Think nothing of it," I said gaily but he hung up.

I seemed to be having my ups and downs in a hurry, I felt sad again. I twisted my wedding ring round and round. I went to the window and looked down, I pushed at it and it flew up as if it were greased, not like at home where you finally gave up and let it stay shut till the hired man chiseled it open leaving big dents and splinters and then in the winter it would be too loose and rattle and shake in half a gale.

I leaned out as far as I safely could, the cool September air trickled down the opening in my blouse, and also chilled my ears. I never saw so many midget people, so many cars. One of those little creatures down there, like headed pins on a map marching in all directions, could be my Derek. I looked up and saw spiraling vapor trails and a pin-point jet that glistened as the sun hit it. Another one was climbing straight up the trail left by the other one like a monkey up a rope. At home the farmer's sons flew low over their fields, zooming over the trees and down again dusting the crops, and the vet flew in and out with medicine for sick cows and ailing calves.

I was grasped from behind by strong lean arms and I felt hard thighs against my soft bottom.

"Derek!" I cried. "Where have you been!"

Instead of letting go he held me firmly, his two hands closed around my hips, and I felt his pelvis come forward as if he were searching for something.

"Derek." I tried to twist around.

"Be quiet," he said, "stay the way you are."

I had been longing for him all morning but I turned cold at this funny approach. It was awkward.

"Let go," I begged.

I felt his chin upon my neck and he was breathing hard.

I hated him, why, he was like a big beetle on my back, anger welled up in me. Did I have to endure it? I suddenly felt only boredom.

"Oh stop it," I said crossly. "I don't like it."

He let go and I dropped my head on my arms over the sill and started to cry. I heard him go away into the bedroom, he did not try to comfort me and the tears ceased at once.

I turned, arranging my skirt, and kicked off the high heels I had put on for him. On the table I saw a bunch of incredibly long-stemmed pale yellow roses wrapped in a triangle of glistening white paper.

"Derek darling!"

"Hello," he said, coming back tucking his tie under his jacket, as if nothing had happened.

I threw my arms around his neck and pressed my-

self close to him, I raised my chin and closed my
eyes and opened my mouth but I got merely a touch
of his lips on the cheek, and his body stiffened, I
could have fallen, he did not support me, he seemed
to be thinking of something else. I opened my eyes
and stepped back. I felt terribly offended and stupid.
I was ashamed.

He looked absently around the apartment. "Do
you like it, Sigourney?" he said kindly.

At the sound of my name spoken so gently by my
beloved I felt comforted. "I love it Derek, it's so *cute,*
but the roses, the lovely yellow roses."

His face lit up, he was pleased, "They aren't as
pretty as your garden roses," he said, and "No," I
said without thinking.

"But you like them?" His smile had faded.

"I love them because they are from you, because
you thought of me wherever you were for so long,
Derek, where *were* you? I'll put them in that blue
vase." I thought of the last September roses at home,
fat buds almost afraid to open against a possible
change of wind, with bright green jackets, mosslike,
supporting them, they had fat stems and big thorns.
These roses looked ailing, their stems scarcely held
up their heads with pale cheeks. Why, there were
even teardrops on their petals! or synthetic dew, I
thought. They were opening fast, you could see them

tremble like in the movies. In an hour they would topple and die and their shriveled petals would have a musty smell, the smell of death. Hothouse roses, I thought, pale and sickly.

"What are you thinking, Sigourney, standing there like Ophelia talking about rosemary," he laughed affectionately, "in your stocking feet?"

I loved him so I put my hand to my throat but I did not risk another rebuff. "I love you," I said solemnly, hanging my head.

"You don't look like a woman in the transports of love," he said, amused, it appeared.

"How do you mean 'transports'?" I said sullenly, I felt a criticism.

"How do you mean 'transports'?" he mimicked.

"What's so funny," I said, really wounded, "what's so damn funny?"

"Oh Sigourney, let's not act like children."

"You mean don't me act like children," I said.

"Watch your grammar, dearest."

"Oh Derek, I'm so *lonely*," I said it without knowing I would say it, it wasn't even so, how could I be lonely? "Derek."

"Yes?"

"Put your arms around me."

"There," he said, "there, don't fret."

"You—you said I didn't look like a woman in the transports of love," I complained, taking advantage.

He pushed me gently away.

"You look very sweet," he said, "like a boy."

"You don't like my hair short."

"I do," he said wearily. Why didn't I shut up? Well, I couldn't.

"I didn't look like a boy in my new nightie," I said, "but you went out and didn't come back, where were you, Derek?"

"I just took a walk."

"On our honeymoon!"

He looked startled. "Why, I was only gone an hour," he said, "and I . . ." he looked at the roses, he was going to say, "I bought you some roses," but he didn't say it.

"Listen Sigourney, I love you, do you understand?"

"I'm not stupid," I said ungraciously.

"You are, a little," he said, very gently.

The telephone rang a third time and he strode across the room to get it.

"It's the wrong number!" I sang out. "We've got the wrong number here!" I felt as if I had won a point.

He hung up the receiver. "You're right," he said. He went over to the window and looked out, it seemed a long time, the electrical equipment hummed and choked, the milk bottles vibrated like bells in the icebox.

3

For fun I guess, Derek, he is a darling really, had our telephone number changed when he went back to work but I rather miss it, it never rings any more and strange voices ask for Peter. But every day Derek calls me once from the office so I won't call him there; he says I shouldn't, and he sounds so cold and distant with nothing to say, just pauses, and I hear typewriters, that it isn't any use, anyway. Once I said, "For God's sake Derek, I'm so lonely, darling, please . . ." and he said, "I'll ask my secretary to make a note of it, good-by sir, thank you for calling." I banged down the receiver before he could and my eyes blurred with tears of self-pity and the carpet all around looked like fog the color of strawberries and cream.

"Sydney dearest, I'm glad you're here now that the

honeymoon is almost over and it was sweet of Derek
to let me send for you even if he does swear when he
has to take you out at night, it's no fun for you either
on a leash, poor darling." Sydney is used to my writing every day and doesn't hear me, she is sound
asleep in the chair with blue roses on it. She doesn't
complain that there are no rabbits to lope after or
woodchuck holes to bury herself to the haunches in,
her tail covered with burrs, or squirrels to bark
absent-mindedly at, not even a cat to turn one's back
on and pretend you haven't seen.

Derek didn't even kiss me the day after our first
night together or try to put his arms around me after
the window episode. He seemed suave and gay, a
perfect gentleman, thoughtful and good like a big
brother and I was content. We went out in the park
and had lunch there in a restaurant and he cooked
the supper, he insisted. It was delicious, a French
omelet that he keeps turning over on itself like a
little blanket and mushrooms, the kind I pick off the
lawns at home, and strawberries in September.

"You're a gourmet," I said.

"Yes I am," he said.

"I want to cook tomorrow, I can, you know."

"There will be plenty of time," he said, "forever
in fact."

I felt queer. "Really?" I said.

"Yes," he said, "I waited forty years, now it's for good. Are you happy?"

"Yes, oh yes," and I took hold of his head, I was standing behind him, but he disengaged himself and went over to the icebox to put away the cream.

I thought of the evenings once a week, which was as often as Mother let him come, when we sat on the couch for hours just holding hands and kissing.

"Let's sit on the couch the way we used to," I said. "Come on," I said, and I took him by the hand and led him in and gently shoved him down. I sat beside him and laid my head on his shoulder. "Kiss me, Derek, no one is looking, Delia's in the kitchen. Daddy won't come in."

Derek didn't fall in with my little game at all. He did lower his head and kiss me once and my early morning desire for him revived, a grown-up desire, a terrible desire. Now we will go to bed, I thought, and do it again, like last night. But he turned up the light and said, "Shall I read to you?"

"Yes," I said doubtfully, "I'd love that." Why not. But this is our honeymoon, I thought, I thought . . . I thought . . . what did I think? Well, I thought a honeymoon meant kissing and making love from morning till night.

"Derek?"

"Yes."

"Do you love me?"

"You little fool!" It came out quick, he hadn't meant to say it, it was terrifying.

"Oh!"

"Come to bed," he said roughly. "I'll show you."

Where was his tenderness? His face looked thin and hard like a ferret's, like a knife, I was frightened, his long hand shot out and he ripped my pretty dress down the front, the pearl buttons bounced off the table under the light.

"Derek," I begged, "my new dress . . ."

"Come to bed," he said softly as if the self-control cost him ten years of his life, "it's what you want, isn't it . . . all day isn't it what you've been thinking of?"

"Yes," I said brokenly.

"Come then."

I walked ahead of him into the bedroom. It shouldn't be planned like this, I thought; I felt nothing more than if he were politely letting me precede him down the aisle at the theater, the terrible sweetness was gone.

"I'll take it off," he said like honey. He neatly undressed me. I wanted to hide but he looked at me, the twin flames in his eyes were like blue lightning. I shut my lids down and heard him taking off his clothes. My heart beat fast, I felt it in my throat, but it was fear, nothing but fear.

"Look at me, Sigourney."

Oh God, I prayed. I couldn't, in my mind's eye I saw what he wanted me to see, primitive and crude, I had seen it before . . . where? I couldn't remember.

I heard him move away; He is leaving me, I thought, going away, oh dear, he is going for a walk. Try, I said to myself, try, open your eyes.

"Derek?"

He put out the light and I sighed. Suddenly I felt him on me, his hands raced over my body, his mouth searching for mine in the dark, he opened my lips and I felt his tongue like a big rough lozenge. For a moment I responded, a thin pain shot through my loins and I raised myself up. I felt him sinking into me, abandoned words came out of his mouth as he raised his head, arched his back and began it.

"No! No!" I cried when my mouth was free. "No I won't."

But he was lost, I felt his loss, he wasn't there, he couldn't hear me, he was a stranger, a strange beast, and I was not Sigourney, my identity was gone.

"Beast!" I cried. Ahh, the tears ran down my cheeks.

He kept it up and I lay lifeless as a corpse.

"I'll finish," he said hoarsely, but he stopped, he waited.

"Derek, I can't stand it," I pleaded. "Wait, wait, I beg you."

All of a sudden it was over. I felt cold as ice, my head pounded, but a real pity came over me, for Derek, not for myself, for Derek the man, as he lay on my breast, inert, for that second that my pity lasted. He got up, I did not look, and I hated him, I hated him terribly, fiercely, I despise you, I said, but not out loud. God in Heaven, everything is over. I hate him.

I needed comfort, I wanted to go home, "Daddy," I whispered. No, Mama, Mama, Delia. I needed a woman, the soft arms, the yielding breast of a woman. Sisterhood I needed, this was the battle of the sexes, Daddy couldn't help me now, if I called him he would send me a check!

The clock in the square rang out, it was only nine o'clock. The long night lay ahead of me. I remembered Derek's "forever" and the fear of foreverness gripped me, it stretched out before me like a long walk to a distant point, no trees, nothing, a horizon that wouldn't be there when I got there and yet I could not die, I could not sleep. I moaned, I did not mean to be heard, I moaned softly, it helped, I could not cry. I was beyond tears, tears were for children, sweet and salty, they nourished the tissues of children only.

"Sigourney." His voice came to me as if from a long ways off, as if he were in a little boat way out on the pond and I on the dock, but it was penetrating, sweet like a caress.

"Sigourney."

I was wide awake and on my guard. I gathered up my defenses such as they were.

"Sigourney little girl, Sigourney Junior," he said.

My lip trembled, the language of Daddy, of the big brown expressman.

"I'm sorry, it won't happen again."

But I couldn't forgive him.

"All right," I said.

"Forget it, will you?"

"All right, Derek." I tried to keep the impatience out of my voice, I longed for sleep, oblivion.

I went to sleep before he did, lying by my side, and I woke up later to hear his deep and even breathing, the sleeping man, captive almost, conquered, harmless, self-subdued.

Then it came over me and I let it. Like soft and overlapping waves at low tide, like wafers of sea water it lapped against me, this desire, I lay on my back with uplifted chin and let it come higher and higher. Derek stirred, I held my breath. If he should wake! The pleasure increased without any subject matter, without Derek! He lay there sound asleep, our bodies did not touch and yet the sweetness mounted me, came toward my breasts.

"Derek!" I cried, I could not help it. "Derek!" To be loved by nothingness without pictures in my brain frightened me and yet it seemed to be marching on, I longed for it.

"Derek!" and I climbed onto him, I kissed his mouth with all my being and he woke at once just in time for the ecstasy to lose its ghostliness, to be real, to be physical, he wasn't a moment too soon.

Again I had found him, taken the initiative, and had almost lost him forever. What an escape!

"What are you up to," he had muttered, but he knew, it didn't take him long to orient himself, he came into the harbor with all the lights on and the band playing. He's a genius!

I felt gay, happy, but some unfinished business nagged at my brain that wasn't actually sleeping during the procreative act. Is it possible? I had hated Derek, I lay alone by myself and desire came to me ... for whom? Suppose I had waited, whose mistress would I have been? What sort of union would it have been, headless, legless, bodyless! I was frightened at my centerless imaginings like a hypnagogic dream just before waking, my gaiety went away. I lay silent and preoccupied and Derek without a word turned on his side and went to sleep.

Pity, pity me, an admiral's daughter she, the Gilbert and Sullivan tune repeated itself over and over in my tired brain, my depth perception waxed and waned, my teeth snapped down hard as my jaws relaxed and I went out like a light.

As I think of us now, afterward, as I look down on us, how like two corpses we must have seemed on a battlefield.

And after a given length of time, while like two hourglasses possibly upended by sleep, the tiny reddish grains, revivifying clean blood, silently built up, cone-shape, within us, we would awaken, as we did, to do it again and forever, none the wiser, every night.

I felt tender and womanly upon awakening and as if I had had a powerful anesthetic, I didn't remember the aches and pains before the operation.

I heard Derek in the kitchen and the pleasant little sounds of breakfast being prepared, and I felt secure and safe, unreasonably so, really.

"Doctor," I called gaily.

He looked in at me. "What do you mean?"

"The operation was a success," I said.

"I don't follow you. Do you want an egg?"

I regretted my facetious remark. It was out of character, not like me anyway, it had connotations, it was almost a dirty joke I thought being a male, he would appreciate.

I never say the right thing, I muttered to myself,

I'm always wrong. But he *is* hard to please, what is the matter with him?

"Why are you staring at me?" I said at breakfast. "Why are you looking at me like that?" I had felt a penetrating questioning look in his dark eyes that he hastily withdrew as I looked up.

"You look very pretty." He was lying. I don't mean I didn't look pretty, I certainly did. "Don't ever look sloppy" was about the only rule I knew to be without exceptions in the married-life catalogue of dos and don'ts and How to Keep your Husband that I had picked up somewhere; for the rest I was ignorant. But that wasn't why he was staring. He was simply looking at me hard while he thought something even harder, the way one does when one concentrates, it helps; I was just an object that held his attention while he asked himself . . . what?

I felt a sickly fear as if I were invisible and it came to me that he was a stranger and I to him a stranger, too, possibly. I wanted to creep into his arms, only the warmth of him, the contact of him, would comfort me. Like a dog I wanted to be comforted by my tormentor, like a child I would creep into the arms of the nurse who had paddled me. I looked at my egg and hit it hard with the spoon. The toast popped out of the toaster and the hot-water kettle let out a shrill prolonged whistle. Derek set it aside and made my tea. The sunlight that never lasted more than fifteen minutes rounded the corner and left us in a funny morning twilight and the first silence of the honeymoon, except when we were sleeping, began.

The egg was tasteless, the toast dry and the tea like medicine; like little marionettes atop a mechanical music box we avoided each other in the tiny kitchenette as we washed and dried the dishes and put things away. How handy he is, I thought, using an expression of my grandmother's, like a woman, Daddy is clumsy and absent-minded, helpless and adorable around the house like a big dog, and Mama purses her lips and puts up with him but what would she do if he took away her prerogatives and canceled her maternal instincts; on the other hand how happy Daddy looked when Mama couldn't add and didn't know the shape of Czechoslovakia; and the biggest compliment he could give her was "Just like a woman," and "Men are so helpless" made him snuggle up in his big leather chair and chuckle, he loved it that way.

"Where is my trunk?" I broke the silence.

"In storage."

"Storage?"

"Come, Sigourney, where else would it be, you won't be needing it for a long time, if ever."

"But isn't it up attic?"

"Darling, there are no attics here."

"Or cellars?"

"No dearest."

"I like my trunk," I said childishly, "I might need it." I closed the icebox door and over my head the electric clock buzzed and the second hand revolved twice before Derek said, "Sigourney," and came up behind me. I spun round as if I feared he held a gun in his hand. I did visualize a weapon.

I didn't miss the pain written on his narrow face before he said quite gently and calmly, "Shall we picnic in the park?"

"Oh yes Derek!" How easily, as I think of it now, he—what is the word?—almost manipulated me. But contented again, I did not look forward to the picnic as I made up our bed where not long ago I had straddled him; what did he mean I would not, perhaps *never*, need my trunk? I stared at the mark of my mouth on the pillow, a red smudge, and at the very bottom under the pink sheets I came upon his pyjama trousers. My heart beat fast at these insignia of intimacy; in the living room, fully dressed, my lover was a stranger, someone who had come to call. I suddenly wanted to prove something to myself, if only to change the subject in my mind.

"Derek, come here," I called.

"Yes?" He sauntered, almost, in, looking around him as if to acquaint himself with the surroundings.

"Derek." I meant it, my feelings canceled the ruse,

"Derek," and I reached my arms, warm soft arms—
I thought, and my hair is over my forehead, so becoming—around his neck. "Derek, I love you, I want
you, now." I put a lilt in my voice not to be too
deathly serious, but I felt a heavenly weakness in my
knees. Now, I thought, this is it. The heat of my passion flew up into my face, I opened my mouth and
could not lift my eyelids from over my rounded
eyes.

"I'm not a mechanical toy," he said. "I'm sorry,"
he added.

"Oh don't be," I cried. "I was joking," and I
forced a grin that must have looked like a crack in a
vase.

"Sigourney, for Christ's sake," he said but he said
it quietly. He looked as if he were in a sickroom and
wanted more than anything to get away, the thin
nostrils flared like a horse's at a paper bag.

As he turned I shoved him, my hand flat between
his shoulder blades, but he stiffened his back and
turned on me. There was the sulphurous blue flame
in his eyes and I had time to think, Anger and love
is the same in his eyes, why? before he grabbed my
two wrists and said, "Behave yourself!"

"It's our honeymoon," I wailed. "I'm not a child,"
and I longed to be, I longed to be rocked and cradled
in his arms.

I have lost all that, I thought.

"I'm lonely," I sobbed.

"Look here," he said, "enough of this." It seemed to me everything he said was an anticlimax; it was like walking down a flight of stairs with no landing in sight.

I made an effort to keep in the mood and stamping my foot, cried, "Go! Go! Go! I hate you."

"Perhaps," he said. Do you see what I mean?

The scene was a failure and I said, "I'm sorry, Derek, I'm terribly sorry." I didn't feel anything at all. The picnic like a picture in a storybook attracted me again.

As I sit here chewing my pencil, Sydney snoring evenly in the big chair, her tail hanging down lifeless as a piece of rope, I am amazed at the big and little compromises and adaptations of life. I had settled for the picnic in the park without any more ado and it was a dear picnic exactly like the picture I had visualized. If I had been nude it would have looked like a Manet, the grass still viridian in September, the bark of the trees dark and steaming, the foliage like little clouds. But the picture has a formality about it and the white napkin spread on the grass between us is a little studied, a little blue, the bottle of wine, amber and transparent in the dappled light, casts too short a shadow for my taste. But

Derek looking straight into the eyes of the observer is as handsome as a Parisien on just such a picnic as this. If I had been nude I would have lolled a little and laid one arching hand along my inner thigh; the flesh tones of my breast and belly, the mauve and delicate shadows in the right places, would make the connoisseurs whistle softly, the landscape would recede, even Derek diminish in his slim black suit and incredibly far away a stretch of blue water compliment even at that distance my reddish curly hair, placed there for just that aesthetic reason.

4

That everlasting formal park with everything in the right place, and no burrs to jump at you as you go by and settle on you like barnacles, no ticks, no moss, no edible fungus like overdone soufflés at the base of great oaks covered with lichen and thick bark like curling waffles. No grasshoppers zoom at crazy angles underfoot, no iridescent dragonflies ride each other's quivering tails just for fun; not even a lizard with a pink tongue and yellow belly, motionless, feasts on invisible gnats. The pigeons are stuffed with cotton and wound up by hand, I'm sure there is a little brass key for each, and the dogs, poor dears, all on leashes, some of them in sweaters, and I saw one with overshoes. At night that man-made moon I read about is up there already but they forgot the lovers, a man and a maid embracing in it; it's tricky

how they get that little padded muslin cloud to pass
over it every hour on the hour, that I must admit.

I took a walk one night alone—"Keep moving,"
said a big cop, swinging his club around and around
his wrist like a kid practicing. He might say, "Bang
Bang, you're dead," or "Pow! Roll over."

"It isn't a good idea to go out at night alone," said
Derek, "in the park."

"I always walk out at night in the country," I said.
"It's so lovely and delicious."

"I don't want you to here," he said quietly. "You're
my wife," he added.

Now what is the logic of that? I thought.

"What could happen to me?" I asked.

"You could be raped," he said. "Do you understand?"

"Oh yes, I understand," I said, I grinned broadly.
"Say it again."

"What?"

"Rape," I said softly, I blushed. "*The Rape of the
Lock*," I added, to re-establish my innocence in his
eyes, they had flickered dangerously. What is the
difference, I thought, between rape in the park and
rape at home? Well, I figured, one is legal, one is
condoned by the Apostolic Catholic Church and the
other is nasty.

"Alexander Pope," I said.

"Yes, I know."

"Let's talk about it some more," I said. "What else could happen to me now that I am your wife?"

"I don't like your sophisms," he said, frowning; his mind is quick, he understood, I thought it was fun but he didn't.

"You don't like them?" I said, and I laid a palm on either breast. "You don't think they're pretty?" It was no good, just silliness, he didn't smile. What shall we do now? I thought. Besides, the gesture had been unseemly, almost vulgar; it was his fault that I kept stepping out of character, I was trying too hard, I'll never get used to him, never relax.

As if he read my mind he said, "You've changed, Sigourney."

"Isn't it a good thing?" I said, the tears coming into my eyes. "Don't you want me to change, you don't love me as I am, you just . . ." I stopped.

"What," he said, "I just what?"

The tone, as of a catechism, startled me, what was the answer?

"You just married me . . ." I couldn't finish, it was as if klieg lights were on me, I couldn't think why he had married me, I had never thought about it, I was completely unprepared.

"Just what are you accusing me of?" he said.

Why *had* he married me? Certainly not for money,

poor Daddy was spending his modest capital, and
not because I was chic and stylish, I'm not glamor-
ous, I'm not brilliant; he didn't marry me to show me
off to his friends.

"Why?" I said, and I really wanted to know, "Why
did you marry me?"

And then it came to me: he married me for *that!*
A word came into my mind, Allyn had used it, it was
one of the lost entries in my little-girl's diary, cen-
sored and come to light again. I shivered.

He was speaking, softly, asking me something.
"Why did you marry *me*, Sigourney?"

"I love you, I love you!" I cried. "I love you, Derek,
that's why!"

He stepped forward but the dirty word plucked
at my intelligence and I cried out my denial. "No no,
Derek! I didn't marry you for *that!*"

Had I?

"What is *'that,'* " said Derek, like an inquisitor;
his lips curved in a smile but there was no amuse-
ment in his eyes.

"Don't brainwash me," I said sulkily. I felt I had
given myself away, I felt that he stood pure and
aboveboard like a clean mast on a ship and that I,
well, I had slipped into a slough of childish nastiness
that he couldn't possibly know anything about. The
word stayed with me, what an escape! I might have,

in my loss of orientation, spoken it aloud. I looked
at him wide-eyed, I have not yet learned to dissimu-
late. Into my consciousness flooded the remembrance
of last night and the language of abandon he had
used, as if I were not there, words I had not recognized, but comparable words? Did he despise me?
Did he sense evil in me? "No no," I said and shook
my head. "Derek?"

"Sigourney darling." He seemed to let go of himself, the tenuousness left him, the *thinness* as if he
were on tiptoe; the inquisitor backed away. "Sigourney darling, let's be happy."

Big stupid I was, I could have walked into his
arms and been reassured, comforted, his funny aloof-
ness had disappeared and he was adorable for just
that minute that I wasted.

"Happy?" I said. "With nothing solved? Nothing
is solved," I moaned. I hung my head and waited for
him to put his arms around me but he straightened
up and resumed, I can only call it, his vigilance. It's
a matter of split-second timing, I said to myself, with
him. Where was my heart? I felt alert and heartless.
I was his match, because where was his? The solu-
tion does not seem to be at hand and it is nearly
time to go to bed.

I write in the present tense as if it were happen-
ing to me now what didn't happen to me that vacant

night, the night of the honeymoon that was lost forever, that dreamless wordless night.

"Goodnight, Sigourney."

" 'Night Derek." I stared straight into the darkness, my eyes were so wide open I could feel the tickle of my long lashes on my upper lids; the man I loved lay deep in sleep, only a tiny bit of warmth came to me from him, I might have been lying on a raft at sea on a moonless night next a dead man. I felt the gentle upsurge of the tide, I imagined light airs and whispering monotonous currents aloft and alow, pale green flora and bits of albino sponge rode the glassy trough, a sob escaped me that almost awakened me but not quite, and it was morning. *It's a pity to waste it with a honey like you.*

I heard someone crying, I said to myself—a woman's stifled sob, could it be Ceceley, my roommate, homesick again?

I oriented myself so fast I almost fell out of bed. I must have appeared in the kitchen door like a doll out of a box, I felt the calcimined look of me, fresh as paint.

"Hello honey," said Derek, he had heard the snap and crackle, like lightning in a handkerchief, of my orlon wrapper that had been charging itself all night on the bed post; he ladled out two boiled eggs. "Did you sleep well?"

"I was unconscious if that's what you mean," I said cavalierly, but I felt good, a kind of happiness pervaded me, I hadn't had time to think. I sniffed the aroma of coffee I had learned to like up my nostrils, and it was cozy and sweet in our tiny kitchenette, the square of sunshine delighted me as if it had been a whole roomful, and the bend of Derek's smooth head, the grace and beauty of his stance, his brownness, the flicker in his dark eyes like a bird's wing almost, entranced me. I couldn't help it, I didn't plan it, I kissed him warmly on the mouth and let go quickly.

"I love you so," I said, and how I meant it, how I meant it!

"You're sweet," he said seriously and looked deep into my eyes for just one second. It was worth it. *There's Honey on the Moon Tonight. . . . Come along and let's taste it . . .*

"Do you mind if I take a walk while you . . ." He made a sweeping gesture that took in the apartment.

"No darling, do take a walk," I said, "do take a walk, darling." I wanted to kiss him again just as warmly and receive the same deep serious look but I guessed it couldn't be repeated, not spontaneously anyway. He reached a long arm into the hall closet and came out with his Homburg between his thumb and forefinger. He gave it an appraising look and

popped it on his head, he lifted his chin, and gave
the brim a slight tug, settling it, and smiled at me.
"So long." But he was already gone, at least a block
away. I didn't like the black Homburg, it's his town
hat, it doesn't suit him, I mean it doesn't suit *me*,
and his shoes, I know they are terribly expensive, but
they are too long and pointed and satiny. He looks
too chic for my taste, like a member of the International Set. How I loved him in the country in an old
tweed jacket and sneakers and no hat. I felt a dis-
tinct nostalgia for the good old days when we were
engaged, last week.

I busied myself with the ridiculous little play-act-
ing chores of our doll's house. I kept an inner eye
on myself and noticed how pretty and domestic I
looked, womanly and charming; I began to sing as
I swished a spotless medicated dustcloth here and
there, *"It's blowin' a gale and a gale and a half and
I don't see fittin' to lower."* The bed was made, the
dishes washed and put away, the dusting all done. I
dressed, picked up my things, kicked my slippers
under the bed, screwed the top on the toothpaste,
gave the shower curtain a shake, stuffed yesterday's
towels in the hamper and hung up fresh ones. I noticed the big red initials S. W. were upside down so
I turned them the other way. *"It's blowin' a gale and
a gale and a half and I don't see fittin' to lower,"* I

improvised a little on the tune, which was my own in
the first place, and synchronized the beat.

I looked up at the electric clock, I raised a pointed
chin, a smiling mouth and candid eyes like a dear
little girl looking up at her mother who holds a present behind her back, and fifteen minutes had elapsed.
"God damn it," I said.

Derek would be gone an hour as usual, I couldn't
refuse him his hour alone but I resented it, and he
knew it. I had been pleased with myself for letting
him go so cheerfully, it had been very sophisticated
of me—Why yes, do go, why not darling, run along.
I flipped the back of my hand at no one. What a
relief to have a moment to myself, men are such a
nuisance around the house.

I looked at the row of books all right side up and
tidy and shining in the two bookshelves behind the
lamp, but they weren't my books and I did not want
to have anything to do with them.

I hung out the window and watched the traffic
but it made me dizzy. "This is a hell of a honeymoon," I said out loud and the telephone rang. It
was the first time since Derek had the number
changed and I hesitated a moment, picked it up
and said, "Hello, wrong number." I meant to beat
whoever it was to it.

"I beg your pardon?"

"Wrong number," I said flatly.

"I'm looking for Derek Wagstaff . . ."

I am, too, I felt like saying but I said, "This is Mrs. Derek Wagstaff," and it made me feel strong and proud.

"How do you do, Mrs. Wagstaff, will you tell Derek Peter called?"

It's still the wrong number, I thought, only Peter's there and not here the way he wasn't.

"Hello?"

"Hello," I said.

"Peter," he said.

"Okay," I said, it wasn't the proper response, it wasn't dignified. He hung up and I returned the receiver to the hook, thinking hard.

I never heard of Peter, I said, I felt jealous, left out of something. Don't be silly, I said, a man has friends. But he never mentioned any Peter. Why, he's never mentioned anyone. I laughed but it was a peakéd, unsuccessful laugh. He's got heaps of friends, I insisted. He knows a lot of women, married women, clever women; I laid it on, I might as well get used to it. I felt very sorry for myself. *Honey, honey honey honey*.

Take it on the chin, be a good sport, I said to myself as if I were my best friend. "But who *are* all these people?" I said out loud. "That's what *I* want to know, what do they look like, calling up my husband in droves, 'Is Derek there? I'm looking for Derek,' " I mimicked. I hung up the imaginary receiver with a crash. "Calling *me* up and asking for *my husband*."

5

Where does Derek walk to all alone? I imagined him tipping his Homburg to every other woman, pretty women, they all looked exactly alike, on the busy avenue, and when the lights changed, they chatted awhile, Derek stood with his hat in his hand because he is a gentleman and the wind lifted a lock of hair over his forehead and the pretty woman watched how the light struck it, burnishing it, and she touched his arm with two fingers of her white-gloved hand to emphasize something she was saying, a reminiscence perhaps, "Do you remember . . ." Think of all the women he must have known, why, he's forty years old; he was twenty when I was born, a mewling infant, yes a mewling infant. I saw myself in a frilly bonnet and a diaper, and white shoes three inches long, steadying myself on the porch and Derek pass-

ing on the other side of the street under the elms
with a blonde girl, a ghostlike girl, featureless, clinging to his arm, she wore heels like stilts and her
hair looked like a hatch of moths floating round her
head, but Derek looked the same, exactly the same.
Had Sigourney Junior marked him as her own, the
mewling infant with the bulging brow who kept trip-
ping over her own feet, top-heavy as a croquet mallet? Thank God he had not looked and seen me then,
how could he ever have gone through with it if he
had?

After the blonde girl, too unreal to upset me very
much, there was probably a married woman, I read
somewhere that married women seduce young men
very easily; I imagined an oldish woman of thirty-
five swinging her hips as Derek followed her all too
willingly into her house, up the steps, and the door
shut behind them, the shades were pulled down, I
saw a plump hand with a wedding ring on it. I was
about five and I rode by in my perambulator, innocent little thing, but pretty now with reddish-
brown wisps of soft hair not yet curling but reaching
out as if they would soon, like young vines looking
for support.

"Baby." Derek came in like an illustration in a
Godey's Lady's Book, carrying like a torch a bunch
of long-stemmed yellow roses.

Yes, that's what he called the woman with mascaraed eyes and him, ten years younger than she, she
called "Daddy." Where did I get such crap? I'm
angry and I want to use harsh words. "Crap," I said
out loud, but not loud enough for him to hear.

"Thank you darling." I had aged, I stood up and
reached for the roses.

"Sweetheart," I said, "the telephone has been ringing constantly." I really thought so, I looked, I believed, exhausted, but interestingly so, like Marlene
Dietrich sipping an absinthe in Venice.

He glanced at the phone (so did I) as if to verify
my statement, there was no sign that it had ever
rung, or would ring, again.

Well, it's my word against its, I said absurdly to
myself.

"Wrong number?" he said, arching his brows, and
for one second I glimpsed an affectation, like a
woman stirring her after-dinner coffee, two fingers
on the tiny hot spoon, and giving her escort a mys-
terious look from under her beaded lashes before she
said, well, nothing.

"No, it was for you—Peter," I said. I wanted to get
on with my arithmetical daydream of how old I was
when Derek was how old, I stared at him wide-eyed
as if I was still in pigtails, when I was ten my nurse
disciplined my curls into fat pigtails because it was

easier that way. Then he would be—I squinted my eyes at him—thirty. What kind of women do men like at thirty? . . .

"Peter?" he said. "What did he say?"

"Nothing."

"What did you say?"

"Nothing, it was very dull."

"Who else called?"

"No one."

"I thought you said . . . Did Peter call more than once?"

"Oh no."

"It must have been a long ring."

"Yes," I said, "I didn't think it would ever stop."

"I'll have to have it fixed," he said and he laughed.

"Who is Peter?" I said. With Derek back in our little living room, his Homburg in the closet, close to me, so handsome, I can't imagine very well and I put away my continued story for another day, the women of all sizes turned their backs and trooped away, But I'm not finished with you yet, I made the mental reservation.

"Just a friend," he was saying. "You will like him, he's not much older than you. But he ought to know better than to call."

Wait a minute, one thing at a time, I thought. "I'll like him?" I said. "Is he coming here?"

"Why yes, I suppose so." Over my dead body, I answered to myself.

"But why should he know better than to call?"

"My friends know I've just been married and that we are on our honeymoon. It would just be better taste to wait awhile," he said. He sounded like my great aunt on Long Island, but I went along with him on that.

"I suppose you have hundreds of friends," I said, *sotto voce.* I stroked the roses, palm up, a few petals dropped to the carpet. I couldn't stand it, I would *not* share him with anyone. "Don't answer," I said sharply, in character again. "I don't want to hear anything about them."

"I've only a few . . ."

"Those women," I said, I knew better, but I went right ahead, "all those women that you made love to, *slept with!*" I stopped, I had startled myself. "Oh Derek!" What would he do, would he strike me? Then I anticipated him. "No no! I don't want to go on a picnic," I said, waving the picnic away with both hands and shaking my head.

"It's raining," he said.

"Which direction do we face here?" I asked Derek. I had not thought of it until it started to rain. The little apartment was like a box-kite on stilts, set up for the time being, portable. It wasn't home, it had no cellar, any time the director might say, "Take it down, the next scene is in the desert." I, too, felt as if I had been transplanted and taken to the city in a pot. But the driving rain was real, elemental, it suddenly gave the apartment a steadfastness in my mind, the rain beat on the bedroom windows only and sideways on the single pane in the kitchen, the living room with all the lights on was in the clear. Without waiting for Derek to answer, I said, "That's southwest," pointing out the living-room window, "and that's northeast," I said, raising my other arm and pointing toward the kitchen. "It's a northeaster," I said with authority. "It will last three days." It had taken a storm to give me back my stance. I felt less uneasy, less afraid.

Derek was watching me with a prolonged and loving look, warm like a steady glowing fire on the hearth.

"My Compass Rose," he said. How lovely! How heart-warming, how tender and compassionate. I felt an almost metaphysical union with him, the palms of my hands felt moist and soft, my heart sounded like the tiny tick of a woman's watch inside a cushion, and my soul responded, ectoplasmic.

"Derek! How poetic," I said. "It will be lovely," I

sighed, "three whole days with the storm outside and us in here so safe and nice, just like home."

A shadow slid over his forehead, no bigger than the span of a moth passing a candle.

"You don't feel at home here, do you, Sigourney?"

"Oh yes," I said. "I do now."

"I've always lived in town, it's home to me, but you are a country girl."

"Yes," I said doubtfully; was it a criticism?

"What would you suggest?" he said all of a sudden.

"Suggest? You mean for dinner?"

"Oh Sigourney, you live in the present, you're happy right this second but in five minutes you will be restless or sad. Perhaps I made a mistake bringing you directly here, we should have done the usual thing and have gone to Niagara Falls."

"I want what you want," I said. "Who wants to go to Niagara Falls?" (*I* did! The vision of all that white water falling off the side of the world thrilled me.)

"I was joking about Niagara Falls," he said, "but some nice place, Hot Springs, or Bermuda." He knows people there, I thought. I saw women in white dresses and bare legs, older women, chic and assured, in high heels, clever women—Derek! Hello! Wasn't there a cave somewhere, a hole in the

rocks, and a big sign ROAD CLOSED FOR REPAIRS?
Honey honey honey honey.

"The grottos," he said, and I jumped, "in Bermuda,
on the beach, lovely, blue water and white sand . . ."

"People?"

"A few."

"What's the matter with *this?*" I said. I looked
around the little place lit up brightly in the daytime,
perfectly ridiculous, but sweet. The northeaster
drenched the window panes and deadened the noise
of the traffic, the building swayed slightly as if we
were on top of a mast, almost a circular motion, two
gulls on a mast in harbor. At home a blind would
break loose and bang all night, but our old house
would nestle into the ground and not give a fraction
of an inch. The water would overflow the copper
gutters blocked with fall leaves and the big oaks
would groan and creak and thrash in the wind.
Paul, Mama would say, are the windows all closed?
Of course they were.

"If you're happy here," said Derek.

"I couldn't be happier," I said. "Derek?"

"Yes?"

"Wasn't it funny that before you had the telephone number changed everybody was calling up
and asking for Peter and . . ." I was sitting close to
him on the couch now, each of us had taken up a

book, I felt him grow still; I can't describe it, but like
a cat who has heard a mouse in the wall, he was
breathing shallowly as if he were listening to something I couldn't hear.

"What is it ?" I said.

"What is what?"

"I thought you heard something."

"Just the rain," he said.

I drew closer to him to rid myself of a slight tremor
of fear.

"It's a front going through," he said.

"It's just a northeaster," I said. "They're all the
same. I like them," but I didn't. I didn't like this one.
I felt an uneasiness in Derek, too. Why is he listening? What is he listening for? Then I realized that he
had been listening to me! Waiting for me to finish
what I was saying. But it was of no importance what
I was saying, what was it? Oh . . .

"Derek, wasn't it funny that before you had the
telephone changed everybody was calling up and
asking for Peter . . . and then Peter called up here?"
What was I going to say next . . . ? "Was it the *same*
Peter?" Derek drew out his cigarette case and lit
himself a cigarette and I lost contact with his still-
ness. He had withdrawn himself completely from
me. He might be sleeping, like last night, I thought.
We slept in the same bed side by side, now we are
awake side by side. I don't *belong* to him, he doesn't

belong to me. I am alone! *Pity pity me, a captain's daughter she.*

"I wish I could have Sydney," I murmured.

He laughed, rather lightheartedly, I thought, as if a small crisis had passed.

"May I have Sydney?"

"What a queer name for a dog," he said in a conversational tone as if the waiter was hovering, his pencil poised, to take our order. Two double rib lamb chops, I thought.

"It just suits her," I said. It was as if we had met for the second time—Are you fond of sailing? I just handle the jib, but I adore it.

"I named her after a Jewish boy in the village, his father was an accountant."

"Oh."

"She had the same brown eyes, as if she had had her feelings hurt but didn't blame anyone, as if she thought it was her own fault. I think maybe dogs think they are Jews," I improvised, but Derek's attention was wandering.

"She didn't like you at first, remember? But it wasn't really that she didn't like you, she thought you didn't like her and she didn't want to be the one to make advances, are you listening? You probably smelled funny, only at first, I mean, from the city, new I guess."

Derek was smiling fondly but not looking really

at me, more at some invisible one behind me—the way I had looked at the boy, the country boy, behind the man, behind the trunk.

"Of course you ought to have your dog when I start back to work," he said. "I was going to suggest it." And that's how I got you, Sydney dear. (No answer.)

"Do you remember how we used to sit in front of the fire in a northeaster," I said, "at home? I wish we had a fire."

"I can't send for it," he said, but there was no impatience in his tone or sarcasm.

"I'm not complaining," I said, I sat beside him wondering what had happened to the intimacy of that time, the precious exciting intimacy, the long hours of caressing and kissing, my mouth was swollen with kissing, my heart beat like a hammer, even and hard, as if I had been swimming the inlet. We stayed up much later than we were supposed to and could scarcely bear to part. I knew the light would shine under Daddy's and Mother's door until I came upstairs. We clung together to the last second, the last instant, goodnight sweetheart, goodnight my darling, goodnight, goodnight, our hands couldn't let go of each other; one more embrace, a long and frantic kiss, clinging and tremulous, his long hands slid down my sides, cupping me at the waist almost meeting there, and then caressed my thighs and up behind me, and I nearly died of pleasure. I moaned and stretched myself up against him like a bow against an arrow, and he smoothly separated my legs with his knee and lowered his head as if it were too heavy to hold up, and I felt the wedge of his narrow face between my breasts. Ah so much, so much all at once, and only a moment more, he must go, it is time, goodnight, he nuzzled my left breast and through my blouse took it in his mouth, he lifted his knee between my legs, "Derek!" I cried and, "Christ!" he said as he let go of me.

"Goodnight."

Weak and disheveled, I would tiptoe up to my room, putting out the lights as I went, and look at my wild self in the mirror, a wild girl with eyes as big as saucers and black as ink, my mouth sulky and wet, open, as if I needed more air. My body was stinging all over as if a whole hive of honeybees had landed on me in their nuptial flight, and my skin was so sensitive I did not want to let the sheet down on it. Naked I lay, exhausted with love, wordless, the passionate looks of Derek imprinted on the retinas of my eyes. Oh that loving face, how he loved me and I him.

And now it seemed to me we sat beside each other with nothing to do, making idle conversation.

"Derek," I said when we went to bed, I felt nothing, "make love to me."

"Gladly," he said and he did, expertly.

But I lay afterward as if tossed on the beach by a heartless tide. This is it, I thought. This is passion. This is what other people do, a kind of shame chilled me; before, we were lovers, unique, secret. In every house, I said to myself, in every block, in every street, in the suburbs, on the outskirts, men and women are doing it, women, I said, woman I mean, I am woman, I am no longer Sigourney, me, myself, virgin, with short hair and long legs, a mole on the back of my neck. And Derek, asleep beside me, he knew all this, he knew it and never told me, ah this is what he married me for. He didn't speak he just did it and I . . . oh no no no. I stifled my denials in the pillow and lost consciousness.

And so every night I said, "Derek make love to me." "Gladly," he said.

Last night, I said, "Do it quick," through my teeth and it only took ten minutes. The hell with it.

6

Well, as I have said, the honeymoon seems to be nearly over, not really of course, honeymoons last a month, I suppose, a year? Good Lord! My husband is at his office. . . . "What is it, Sydney?" Sydney gave a voluptuous growl in her sleep. Poor little bitch, I thought, but no, look at her, the long tail is wagging furiously, she bares her teeth and shudders all over. "Wake up Sydney!" What? she looks at me sheepishly and lowers her ears apologetically. "It's all right, good girl, go back to sleep."

But who will comfort me?

"Operator, I want to make a personal call . . . Mrs. Paul Sigourney Logan . . ."

"Hello, Mama?"

"Oh I'm wonderful. Everything is lovely. No it isn't snowing here. It is? How is Daddy? Oh give him

my love and Derek sends his love. Oh yes, Mama,
I'm so happy. Yes I've worn it a lot, it's just right. Yes,
Mama, I sleep very well. No, only the first night the
noise bothered me, I'm quite used to it now. Sydney
is right here, she hated it at first but what . . . Oh no
Mama. I use Fannie Merritt Farmer's cookbook and
besides Derek loves to cook and we go out quite
often, yes I will be careful, I know what you mean,
but we only go to nice places. Well good-by Mama.
Perhaps for Christmas, yes, but Derek is awfully
busy. Good-by Mama. Yes, good-by."

"Hello Mr. Wagstaff please, Mrs. Wagstaff is calling. Thank you. Hello Derek? I just wanted to say
your mother called. . . . Yes darling, I know you will
but I thought I'd forget to tell you, and Derek, we're
having chops for supper. Darling, please listen, the
butcher was horrid to me, he acted as if I didn't
know what I was talking about, he said . . . oh *all
right,* Derek, *good-by.*"

"Come on Sydney, let's go out." Sydney made
half-circles, she reared like a horse, but I got the
leash on her and we took the service elevator to the
ground floor.

Outside she got down on her stomach and
squirmed across the sidewalk. "Sydney, stop it, stand
up," I said.

"What kind of a dog is *that*?" said a little boy.

"It's a hound dog," I said.

"It's a hound dog," he said to his mother, and his mother said, "Come along, don't stare."

"Sydney it's a red light. Sit! Sit, Sydney!" I leaned over and pushed her rear end down hard. "Sit!" I said. She collapsed and rolled her eyes and let her tongue out as far as it would go.

"The light's changed," said a man's voice beside me.

"Oh thank you," I said. "Come on Sydney, look Sydney, come on, let's go, sic 'em Sydney! look! what's that? Come on Sydney." I dragged her across the street on her stomach.

"She doesn't want to go," said a man on the other side, "does she?"

"Oh yes she does," I said. "She's just funny about it."

I picked her up in my arms. "Sydney, for Heaven's sake, everybody's looking at you."

"Is your dog in pain?" said a woman with big black eyes and an umbrella.

"I should say not," I said. "She can't wait to get to the park."

"Has he been inoculated against hepatitis?" she persisted.

"She's a girl," I said.

"Has your bitch been inoculated against hepatitis?" she said firmly, looking me in the eye.

I flushed. "Leave us alone," I said. "She's perfectly

healthy, too healthy almost. She doesn't like you," I
added, and I shook Sydney to make her look alert
and mean; she was drooping comfortably in my
arms, I thought I looked like Jesus with a lamb.

"I ought to report you to the S.P.C.A.," the woman
said nastily, but her attention wandered to a Pomera-
nian in a scarlet sweater and I took Sydney over to
the grass, set her down, and told her to hurry up.

I sat on a bench and she came over and looked up
at me admiringly.

"May I sit down?" said a man's voice.

"Of course," I said.

"Would you like a cigarette?" He held out a cigarette case and smiled at me. He was rather good-
looking, quite nice, I thought, he leaned over and
made as if to pat Sydney on the head, he curved his
hand, there was a big ring with a moonstone on it,
but Sydney lowered her head way down and he
patted nothing.

"Oh no thank you, I just took my dog to the park
but she isn't used to the city, she hates it, she doesn't
understand it at all, it seems to her perfectly ridiculous to have to be on a leash and wait for lights to
change and that woman, do you see that woman over
there? she was very rude to her and Sydney is sensitive, at home . . ."

A handsome cop, his buttons and badge shining in

the sun, sauntered over, he said nothing, but twirling his stick around his wrist, he fixed my new friend with a hard cold eye and made a gesture with his head toward the street. The man got up and left. The cop watched him go and then turned to me, he coughed discreetly behind his hand. "Better not *sit down* in the park," he said, he touched his cap and wandered off whistling, his lower lip sticking out.

"Come on, Sydney, it's crazy here, let's go home. Heel!" I said and to my amazement she did, her nose at my ankle. "Good girl," I said, "good girl Sydney," and I ran while the mood lasted and the light was green across the street. But in the service elevator again she straddled her legs and hugged the floor, her ears close to her head and her eyes wild with terror, as we shot up to the top landing. Home, I had called it, for the first time, and as I opened the door with my key, I smelled my own perfume and felt at ease. It was a dear place, like a new coat.

Sydney gave a sonorous growl like something boiling on the stove and stopped short at the living-room door, the hair stood up along her spine.

"Sydney, what is it? Don't be silly," I said.

"Hello!" A young man came forward, a highball in his hand.

Was I in the wrong apartment? "Oh," I said, "I'm sorry, I must be in the wrong apartment," but as I said it I saw the yellow roses, the pink carpet, my own red scarf on the back of a chair. If Derek's Homburg is in the closet, I thought, that will clinch it. I opened the door, it wasn't there because Derek was out but I could imagine it, a black blob, very dignified and still, I was satisfied.

"Sigourney?" the young man said, in the softest voice I ever heard.

"Yes," I said doubtfully as if I wasn't sure.

"I'm Peter," he said, he had set his highball down and was caressing Sydney, who rolled over and exposed her pink stomach and the double row of her little black tits.

"Get up Sydney!" I said.

"She's a nice dog," he said. "I'm Peter," he repeated.

I looked at him, stared, I'm afraid, I always stare. He looked about nineteen, but not like the boys at home of that age. He had a gentle dignity, a stance, I can only call it, like a little prince, someone who ruled in a little kingdom. A melancholy prince, I thought, there was a slight droop to the mouth although the lips were full, but it was definitely not a pout, it gave him a forlorn look, *Il Penseroso* I remembered. I looked at his reddish hair, tufted like mine and it hung over his forehead like mine, and his eyes, deep and soft, brown as a woodchuck's, were

my own! I lowered my deep soft brown eyes in confusion. His beauty was my beauty, my heart went
out to him.

"How did you get in?" I said coldly.

"With my old key," he said, and he took it out of
his pocket. "I came to give it to you," he said, he held
it out to me and I noticed his round slim wrists and
long hands, paler than mine, stronger.

"Oh I don't need it," I said, still staring at him,
"I've got my own." Don't interrupt me, I thought,
until I finish looking. He was like a drawing done in
white crayon on white paper. As he bent to reach for
the highball I noted the short nose, the softly pointed
chin and the curling lashes, and I felt as if I had
turned *my* head to look in a hand mirror at *my* profile. I longed to kiss him as I had my own glassy
image when I was a little girl alone in a room. The
kiss, long since wiped away, had left its misty print
on my memory.

"Perhaps I shouldn't have helped myself to a highball," he said as if of course he should have, why on
earth not. He's braver than I, I thought, he's not
timid, I'm timid. "Can I make you one?"

"Yes," I said, "except . . ."

"Except what?"

"I don't usually."

"I'll make it weak."

"Oh no, make it strong, I've had a beastly day." I don't know why I said "beastly," I'd never said it before, I usually said "lousy." "Beastly," I repeated, I liked it, and I felt happy.

"What fun," I said.

"Isn't it?" he said, but he did not smile, so I laughed out loud and then he did.

"Ugh," I said and I shuddered as I took a big gulp of the highball. "It's good, isn't it? I suppose you came to see Derek," I said, suddenly remembering Derek whom I waited so impatiently for each day, longing for his return, and whom I had forgotten completely.

"Oh no," he said, "I came to see you, I wanted awfully to see you." He looked at me frankly, almost candidly, but as if a veil were over his eyes like a dog's sometimes when they first wake up, a curtain. "Derek told me I couldn't come until after the . . ." he hesitated ". . . after the honeymoon." I thought he flushed, a little warm color seemed to come into his face but it was as if he were a child going to cry.

"That was horrid of him," I lied.

"Oh no," he said, "I understood," but I thought I saw the sweet lip curl just a fraction, a hint of disgust, it only lasted a split second.

"May I have another?" he said.

"Oh do, help yourself."

"Derek said you read a lot of books and that you liked to draw," he said in a funny way, almost cold. He looked annoyed.

"There wasn't much else to do," I said, "in the country." Why did Derek tell him about me? What did he mean talking about me? It seemed an invasion of my privacy, *our* privacy. Did he tell him about our kisses and caresses?

"I draw awful," I muttered.

"I saw something you did, of him," he said, "and it was very good. He gave it to me."

"He gave it to you!"

"Yes," he said softly, but there was a bridling, a something, I felt we were enemies. Derek had given him the drawing, the little portrait I had so painstakingly made, my heart full of love, my eyes devouring him, my hand shaking, wanting so to set him down on paper, to imprint his loving face forever; and I had succeeded, it was wonderful, it was Derek in love, in love with me. It was an intimate passionate portrayal. My throat swelled in indignation like a snake's, the tears hung on my lashes.

I heard the soft voice saying, "What is the matter?"

I shut my teeth, I got hold of myself, and raised my chin, I looked at him. "Nothing," I said. "I can't draw a bit." But I glimpsed, preoccupied as I had been, hazy as my vision through the unshed tears, a look that passed quickly from his face, but I saw it. It registered and I put it away.

"He didn't tell me you were so . . . pretty . . . beautiful," he said, and the mouth drooped again, the near flush came.

I thought it would be going too far to deny it. I didn't. But I wondered if Derek didn't think I was pretty. But he used to kiss my face and throat and say, "You're so beautiful . . . so beautiful"; that was long ago, before the honeymoon. . . . I grew so silent and absorbed in my memories that I was afraid he would see the pictures in my mind.

"How did you happen to have a key?" I said lightly, I had not really wondered about it, I had been so taken up with his beauty, but as soon as I said it, I did wonder. This is *the* Peter, I said to myself.

Before he could answer I cried out, "You used to *live* here! Why, people were always calling you up. I couldn't imagine who Peter was, 'Hello is Peter there?' all the time. I told them they had the wrong number and then *you*, Peter, called and asked for Derek! How funny! Why didn't Derek tell me you used to live here? Or didn't he know?"

"I live at home with Mother," he said, and he lowered his eyes as if he were going to sleep. A look of fatigue came over him. He began to look as if he weren't there at all, that's the trouble with white crayon on white paper, I thought, only children do that. Sydney raised her head and peered at me near-sightedly the way she does when I talk to myself. Then she wrinkled her nose and gave an audible sniff. She smells his weariness, I thought.

"Peter?" I said softly, I loved saying it but at a loss for going on, I said, "Would you like another?"

He stood up and stared at me the way I had stared at him; was he, too, comparing notes? Did he recognize me? I returned his stare almost impudently, the two of us lowered our pointed chins and from under the tufted thatch of our reddish hair looked into each other's deep brown eyes, and then deeper like going down stairs, deeper and deeper, until I thought I saw in the deepest depths like the bottom of a well, my own image reflected in his wet black pupils, there must have been two of me but I saw only one. I could hardly bear it, I raised my hands palms upward, I was pleading with him. He did not stir, but his lips opened a little. I took two steps forward over the rosy carpet as over a cloud and raised my chin and I felt his mouth on mine, warm and adorable. I took a deep breath and clung to his mouth, he did not support me with his hands, it was as if we were disembodied and the warm sting of his lips was all I knew. The heat of it got into my eyes. He let go and I stepped back.

The apartment darkened suddenly and Sydney snored evenly.

"I'll put on the light," I said, my voice sounded thin as if it came from the corner of the room just over the lamp. He might as well go, I thought. Until the sting of his kiss leaves me, I cannot think.

"When may I come again?" he said, his voice strong and vibrant. "Tomorrow?"

"Oh no," I said, but I meant *yes*.

"I will see you tomorrow then," he said, "and here is your key, it doesn't rightfully belong to me any more."

"Keep it," I whispered, I meant also, *Use it*. My heart beat as fast as a robin's. Sin! I thought.

"Then you must give me yours," he said in a low voice. "This one is no longer mine."

We exchanged keys.

7

I felt gay after Peter left. But before I moved an inch from where I was standing, my chin uplifted, my lips round and full from his kiss, I listened for the elevator. I heard the door slide shut and the hum of its descent. I ran to the foolish little window in the kitchenette, shoved it up and stuck out my head, in hopes of getting a last glimpse of him but I couldn't tell: someone came out and turned right and someone turned left, another someone hailed a taxi and a fourth crossed the street and went into the park. I've lost him, I thought. I felt a cold fear but it went away, I closed the window.

"Sydney, isn't he adorable!" I hugged Sydney and kissed her. "Sydney—" I shook her "—isn't he adorable!" Sydney looked embarrassed. "Let's go out," I said, but Sydney didn't want to go out. The front

door opened and closed. Derek! It was the first
time I hadn't been waiting for him in vain. I always
wait for him in vain and then he comes.

"Sigourney."

"Derek."

I don't know why I didn't kiss him and he made no
move to kiss me.

"I'm sorry I'm late."

"Oh."

"What do you mean 'oh'?"

"I thought you were early."

Derek went into the hall and thrust his Homburg
into the closet on the top shelf and came back; I
mean, I visualized him thrusting his Homburg onto
the top shelf.

"I'm glad you're getting sensible, Sigourney," he
said.

"Sensible? Me?"

"Yes you," he laughed. "It's a strain on a man to
think someone is waiting for him."

"Derek!"

"I'm not used to keeping a woman waiting."

"What woman?" I said. "Do you mean me?"

"Who else," he said.

"Then say me, say 'you,' say 'Sigourney.' Why do
you have to talk in groups? All those women."

Derek gave me an impatient look. "I think I'll have a drink," he said.

"Why don't you like women?" I said. It didn't make any sense but I said it.

There was a short silence, I suppose I sort of confused him.

"What are you talking about?" he said.

"I mean why don't you like *me*?"

Derek looked at me; he reached out his hand and ruffled my hair as if I were someone else's kid on the street. I drew back.

"You're adorable," he said.

"Oh Derek, I'm sorry."

"Forget it, get me a drink."

"But you never drink before your martini before dinner, why do you want a drink?"

Without answering, he went over to the little bar arrangement and looked in the ice bucket, but as he passed Sydney, he shoved her; Sydney looked up at him with big accusing eyes and then she looked at me, Are you going to allow it? she said.

"Derek!" I said. "Don't kick Sydney!"

"Calm down, I didn't kick her. Where's the ice?" He picked up one of the two highball glasses and sniffed at it.

I laughed. "You look like a cat," I said, and he did.

"Who's been here?" said Derek.

"Who?" I said. I had really forgotten Peter, it seemed long ago that Peter was here, it was as if he were someone I had known when I was very young, before Derek.

"Peter," I said, I was talking to myself but I said it out loud. It wasn't a statement or an answer, it was more like a question.

"Peter?" I said again because he stood so still as if expecting to be asked a question. I heard the traffic in the street between the two times I said "Peter."

"What Peter?" he said and he sounded stupid.

I laughed. "Are there groups of Peters, too?" I said. "All those women, all those Peters. What Derek?" I said. "Which Derek? What Peter?" I mimicked.

"Shut up!" He said it loud.

Sydney crept out of the chair and went into the kitchen.

"Don't go Sydney!" I called as if I needed help, a witness, and it looked almost as if I did. Derek stepped forward and laid his hands on me.

"Don't touch me!" I cried dramatically, I had heard it somewhere, someone cried out, Don't touch me!

Derek wrapped his long hands around each of my skinny arms, they felt so skinny and sad, and thrust his face, it looked like a knife, so close to mine that I couldn't focus on him.

"I can't see who you are," I wailed. "Let go of me,
you're hurting me whoever you are."

He let go.

"I asked you a civil question," he said coldly.

"I know it," I said. I tried not to cry, I swallowed
my tears.

"Then answer it."

"You asked me what Peter, how can I answer that?
How do I know which Peter or what Peter? There
was *a* Peter here, that's the Peter who was here. I've
already told you Peter was here. Why do you keep
asking?"

"What did he want?"

"He wanted to see me."

"You?"

"Me, Sigourney, myself."

"Any other reason?"

"He said he wanted to return his key."

"What did you say? His what?"

"I said he said he wanted to return his key, there it
is on the table, there's his what on the table."

Derek became very silent, the way he can. He
stayed that way.

I had a feeling he might kill me, but I said, "Don't
you want to know the rest?"

"The rest?"

I stared at him; why did he look frightened as if he
had had bad news. I hadn't told him yet, how could

he possibly know. And I didn't mean to tell him
either, I don't know why but it was a secret, that kiss.

"Oh nothing," I said. "He just gave me his key because he said it wasn't his any longer, so to be nice I
gave him mine, I don't need two keys."

Derek was listening so hard, his expectancy was so
strained I didn't understand what was wrong with
him. Did he suspect me! Me, his little Sigourney!

"A pretty little scene!" Derek sneered. "A pretty
little scene! Charming!" He was pale. "The little
beast!" he snarled.

"Derek!"

"Sneaking in here!" He seemed beside himself,
like two people almost.

"But Derek, you said he was nice, you said I would
like him. Derek, why are you so upset?"

"You little fool!" he said, he said it like ice, he
filled the glass with ice and the ice snapped, it was so
cold.

I burst into tears. "I am a little fool," I said, "oh
yes, and he is a beast, oh yes, and I hate you!"

"And is that all?" he said.

"What do you mean 'is that all'?" I was interested,
could he have seen us?

"Sigourney," he said.

"Yes? Yes Derek."

"You are lying."

"I haven't said anything," I cried. "How can I be lying when I haven't said anything, I haven't said a thing!"

Then he said, like velvet, like a caress, like a kiss, "He kissed you."

"No!"

"He kissed you," he said.

"No! No!" I denied it, and I wasn't lying. "I'm not lying," I said.

"He is the liar," said Derek.

"Did you see him going out?" I said. "Did you speak to him?"

"No."

I wondered.

While I was wondering he came close. He took me again by the arms, but gently. "Peter," he said.

"Peter?"

He looked, *gazed* is the better word, at my thatch of reddish brown hair, into my deep brown eyes, at my soft and sulky mouth, and he pulled me close and kissed me, a long kiss, the sweetest kiss he ever gave me, the purest, the dearest, full on the lips.

He let go of me.

"Peter," I murmured.

"What?" he said. "What did you say?" he asked quietly.

"Derek," I said, "dear Derek, I just said 'Derek,'"
and I believed I had.

Sydney appeared in the kitchen door. "It's all
right, Sydney," I said, "come on in."

"I wish you wouldn't talk to that dog as if she were
real," said Derek crossly.

"Oh Derek, please, be nice to Sydney. And
Derek?"

He didn't answer; he stood by the window looking
but not seeing in another of his silences. He lit a cigarette.

I went up behind him and put my hand on his arm.
"Please Derek, don't be jealous."

He gave a queer jerky laugh, he turned and faced
me.

"Don't be."

He studied me carefully. I thought he was going
to speak. I waited and I in my turn studied him. I
watched his mouth and I saw the curl of his upper
lip. I looked at, rather than into, his eyes and besides
the square reflection of light from the opposite window, not real light but the light of a city at night, I
saw . . . contempt. That's what it was.

He spoke. "Leave me alone and I'll leave you
alone."

"What?"

"Leave me alone and I'll leave you alone."

"Oh."

"Do you understand?"

"I understand," I said, but I didn't. Finally I said, "I won't ever see him again, I promise you, Derek, I won't ever see him again," and as I said it, I said it a third time with feeling, I really meant it.

Derek said, "I want you to go to Bergdorf's to-morrow and buy yourself a cocktail dress. Charge it." He put out his cigarette in the ash tray as if he meant to burn a hole in someone's flesh—mine?

We didn't make love last night, neither of us wanted to. Sydney wet on the rose carpet without complaining because I forgot to take her out. I sup-pose I ought to be proud, proud as a woman, I mean, that Derek is so fiendishly jealous but I don't feel the way I am supposed to at all. How am I supposed to feel? And a new dress? As if I were a child! But it turns out that the new dress is for the party.

"But I have a dress," I said, "the pink lace one, the one in my trousseau that I've never worn."

"Something more sophisticated," said Derek, "something chic, I don't mind the expense. Black I think."

"I do," I said. "It's against my nature to be extrava-gant. What will I do with two dresses!"

"Buy it to please me," said Derek gently.

"Oh yes, Derek, I will, but black?"

"I'll go with you," said Derek. "I'll meet you at Bergdorf's. Black is very smart."

So Derek and I went shopping. I hadn't been shopping since I bought the filmy nightgown that was so out of character and didn't work and now I was going to buy something chic, sophisticated. Why does Derek want to disguise me?

"Derek, do I have to buy a sophisticated dress and must it be black?"

Derek raised his Homburg, but to whomever it was, she was gone, gone away on her high heels. Derek took, not so much took, as touched, my elbow as we crossed the street, but I eluded his guidance and strode across in my flat heels. All the other women made running little steps with their bottoms sticking out and an anxious little frown on each face. On Fifth Avenue Derek and I got a lot of attention, the women stared at Derek and I stared at them and they stared at me. I suppose I looked like a country girl even in my good suit and what was I doing with the International Set?

"But my dear, it doesn't do a thing for you," said the saleslady.

"No, it isn't right," she said with a tragic air.

"Oh," she said, standing on tiptoe and putting her finger to her lips, "I have just the thing for you! Isn't she sweet," she said to Derek as she lit out of the fitting room.

"Oh my God, Derek," I said, "I'm tired."

Derek laughed. "You look adorable," he said as I stood in my slip and stared disconsolately into the mirror.

"Then why don't you like me as I am?" I said. "Why do I have to have a sophisticated black cocktail dress?"

The saleslady zipped me into something black and slinky, it smelled delicious. I was astounded. I looked divine.

"But your bra!" said the saleslady. "Let me call Miss Anna, your bra just isn't right."

"I'm not going to take off my bra here," I said, I was sorry I said it, I felt so stupid.

"Oh I'm sure your friend won't mind, will he?" said the saleslady, she arched her thin penciled eyebrows.

"He's my husband," I said.

"Oh," said the saleslady, "would you like to step outside, sir?"

"My dear, I thought he was your boy friend," she said as she came in with a lacy bra. "A very handsome gentleman." It was clear she didn't believe he was my husband. "And such good taste," she said, "you're very fortunate."

I didn't think so at the moment but I didn't say anything.

"Now! Sir, come in!" she called. "We have a surprise for you. Stand on tippy-toe so he'll get the effect," she said. "No, here, try these heels," and she set down a pair of high-heeled slippers for me to step into.

Derek looked me over.

"Yes," he said, "and no."

"But sir, she looks simply divine, so chic!"

"I love it," I said.

"Isn't she sweet!" said the saleslady. "And the frock is so smart."

And I'm a fool, I thought, is what she means.

"Just here," said Derek, "the line is not quite right." He was very serious. "And here," he said, "a slight dip, isn't there? and the length is not quite . . ."

"How right you are, sir, I'll call the fitter, these are slight, very slight alterations."

"I like it the way it is," I said. "I'm so tired."

"Oh, poor Madame," said the saleslady, "but how right Monsieur is." I don't know why she changed into French. "Monsieur has an eye."

"And her stockings are the wrong color," said Derek.

"Oh, oui, oui, monsieur," said the saleslady, "but yes."

"Now," she said, as I stood again in front of the mirror in sheer black stockings. "Ahhh! A work of art! Monsieur is an artist. And with Madame's pearls," she said, "when Madame puts her enormous pearls around her neck, such a pretty neck . . ." She acted it out as if putting a string of big pearls around her own neck.

"I haven't any pearls," I said.

"But you will have; Madame will surely have big cultured pearls, they're so smart," and I thought she gave me a predatory woman-to-woman look. If you don't have them before the sun sets, you're a little idiot, her look said.

On the way home I thought about the enormous cultured pearls and I longed for them.

"I don't want any old cultured pearls," I said to Derek. "They're for the birds."

Derek laughed. "I like you the way you are," he said.

"Then why?" I said, stopping in my tracks.

"Ooops! Sorry!" The young man had crashed into me. "Do forgive me," he said, but he was looking at Derek.

"Oh, it's all right," I said.

The young man stared boldly at Derek. "Would you have a light?" he said.

Derek froze. "No," he said.

"Never mind," said the young man. "Cheerio."

"Derek," I said in a loud whisper, "is that a fairy?" I giggled.

"Don't be vulgar," said Derek.

I stopped short again but I looked behind me first. "My word! There are two more of them exactly the same."

"Come on," I took Derek's arm, "let's run."

Derek was furious. "Behave yourself in public," he said.

"Derek!" I wailed. Two women in mink stoles and big alligator bags swinging on their arms looked at each other and smiled.

"I don't care!" I said. "I don't care!" I couldn't see where I was going because of the tears in my eyes.

"Behave," said Derek, taking my arm and pressing it hard till it hurt.

"I *am* behaving!" I said. "This is me and this is the way I behave, take it or leave it."

"Really!" said Derek.

"Really," I mimicked, "really, really." I felt hysterical. "Fancy that," I said, "trick or treat."

"I'll leave you here," said Derek, raising his Homburg, "I've a few letters to sign at the office."

"Cheerio!" I said, giggling. "Cheerio, Fatso," but
he was gone, the light changed and I just stood there,
I saw him, slim and elegant, disappear ahead of me
like a needle in a haystack.

I wonder what he meant, "You leave me alone
and I'll leave you alone," I said to myself. I was calm
again now that he was gone away ahead of me to
sign some letters at the office. Is he really signing
some letters at the office? I asked myself. What make
of woman is he interested in now at forty? I no
sooner thought it than I saw her coming toward me.
She was very beautiful. How old was she? She came
along as if she ought to be on the deck of a ship, I
don't know why, maybe the Azores, I thought. She
walked gracefully and with perfect balance on her
very high heels, her legs were long and slim and she
wore sheer black stockings Ahhh! and a smart black
suit, on one lapel a big emerald brooch, and around
her neck that was long but plump, not skinny like
mine, two strands of enormous cultured pearls.
"Two!" I said out loud, even smarter than one. I felt
like a country lout as the beautiful woman crossed
the street in no agitation at all at the traffic, the taxis
that crowded everyone else, even bumping them, the
scurrying crowd, even a delivery boy on a bicycle.
I was thinking so hard and fast and looking so in-
tently that she seemed to come toward me in slow

motion to give me plenty of time. Her profile passed mine very close but I took in her charming face, smiling almost to itself as if in a mirror. A clever face but not too clever, not like a knife, a face that could hold the attention for a long time, a woman superior to the men who adored her, men like Derek?

"Marie!"

I couldn't help turning to watch.

"Dear boy," said Marie.

The dear boy was Derek's age. Marie was no age at all, no one would dare say she might be sixty. She was just no age at all, ageless, with a terrible attraction. She was adorable, she looked like a picture on someone's piano, royalty. I felt jealousy like a knot in my throat. Ahhh! Here was Derek's woman and fifteen years older than he. How did I know? The dear boy held off his Homburg at an angle like a parasol, catching his death of cold, all traffic seemed to come to a standstill, but he replaced it at a gesture from Marie, things began to move again and he fell into step beside her. I glimpsed his pointed shoes; a member of the International Set. He was almost as handsome as Derek, he could easily be Derek.

So, I said, there is my rival. What chance have I? No more than that little girl in pigtails would have had with that woman of thirty-five with the wedding ring on her finger when Derek was seventeen.

Not until I reached our apartment house entrance
and the doorman saluted me did I remember it was
tomorrow. Peter!

"A young gentleman to see you, madam," said
the elevator man, the elevator man and I are friends.
"Your brother?" he said. "He looks just like you."

"Yes," I said.

"Peter," I moaned; as far as I was concerned it
was still yesterday.

"What is it?" he said coldly.

"Sydney!" I sat down on the floor and hugged
Sydney.

"Mrs. Wagstaff," said Peter.

It meant nothing to me, I went on hugging Sydney. Finally I said, "Who?"

"I have come to say good-by."

I stood up and kicked off my shoes, I crossed the
rose-colored carpet to where Peter stood, a highball
in his hand. I remembered yesterday's kiss as if I had
kissed myself in the mirror. Peter set the highball
glass down carefully and took me in his arms and I
felt a terrible disgust creep over me, I trembled, but
I raised my chin for yesterday's kiss. His mouth was
cold. I stepped out of his embrace and lifting my
hand, I slapped him, the softness of his cheek infuriated me, I slapped him again, hard. Tears came into
his brown eyes and into mine as well. I had lost my

womanhood, I felt insulted. I raised my hand again
but I couldn't bear to touch him. The mark of my
slap painted his cheek crimson. He looked very beautiful like an angel.

"Punish me," he said and he closed his eyes, his
long lashes quivered, his lower lip protruded like a
sullen child's. "Punish me," he said again. "Call me
a little beast."

"Little beast!" I cried before I could stop myself.

"Strike me," he said.

I wanted to say a dirty word, one of Allyn's words,
but I couldn't, I was neither child nor woman, all I
could think of as I calmed down was: He's crazy.
And then I said, "You little fairy!" I was astounded
that I said it. Had I said it out loud? What did it
mean?

Peter didn't move, but he was losing his aura, he
no longer looked like an angel. He said nothing.

"I think you had better go," I said, in a well-bred
voice, like a lady. I saw him glance at the couch that
was directly behind me.

Oh no you don't! I thought, had I read his mind?
Not quite. As I hesitated which way to step aside,
I was off balance and he only had to tap me on the
chest to seat me. Still off balance, he easily laid me
down. Then he ducked his head into my shoulder
and began nibbling my neck, my legs were free, this

was no attempted rape. I felt his warm lips and his
cold teeth. It was like a child that is too old still suck-
ling his mother. I remembered Delia's friend in the
kitchen with her long child in her lap, her breast
bare—"Ouch sweetheart, you're hurting me."
     "Stop it!" I said. I shivered.
     That's when he let go of my neck and flipped me
over, I felt strangled, my face in the pillow, my bottom unprotected, I thought it was bare, I saw it in
the bedroom mirror naked. *Rock of ages cleft for me*
went humming through my head and my prayer was
answered. Peter stood up quickly and I turned over
and sat up as the front door opened and shut. I could
not help but see Peter's hand on himself, although
I averted my eyes, my soul, my essence, from the
ignominy and said it wasn't so.
     Derek seemed to be taking his time thrusting his
Homburg into the closet, maybe he did it twice,
three times, why? Peter had plenty of time to put
the ice in the glass and look like an adorable little
gentleman again, and I sat up straight and in order,
my lips apart, as if I had just said, or was just about
to say, something clever, and as Derek came in I said
it: "Derek darling, where *have* you been!"
     At the end of Derek's long arm—He looks like a
monkey, I thought—clenched between thumb and
forefinger was the hateful Homburg. I almost lost

my poise at this sign of Derek's loss of his. But seeing
my wide-open eyes fixed upon it, he tossed it on a
chair.

"Hello Peter, my boy," he said, but he made no
move toward him, did not really look at him, he simply seemed to know he was there. He spoke in a
fatherly tone. He was acting and rather well and I
could, too.

"Greetings, my love," I said. "A drink?" I thought
what a really good bitch I'd make, deceive my husband and not by a gesture or bat of an eyelash betray
myself. I began to feel better. But what took all that
time in the hall? He's furious, the elevator man told
him my brother was here and he knows I have no
brother. He's fiendishly jealous, he took the time to
control himself, or did he hope to hear something
damaging? Was he listening? But neither did Derek
by a gesture or bat of an eyelash betray himself.

"You're looking well," he said coolly to Peter as
Peter handed him a drink, and he still didn't look at
Peter.

Peter didn't say anything, he even sulked, he stuck
out his lower lip and let his chin drop, but I was
watching Derek, and I noticed something I couldn't
quite place, the expression on his face, and yet I did
—"You look adorable," he had said to me as he
ruffled my thatch of reddish brown hair. Would he

put out his hand and do it to Peter? How perfectly
silly, of course he didn't.

Peter looked at Derek.

"I'm going," he said, "I just came to . . ."

"Never mind," said Derek, "there's no need to explain, my wife is a very attractive woman." He smiled
but I thought the smile a little off-center as if his
teeth were on edge. This is a damn good play, I said
to myself.

". . . to return the key," Peter finished and he raised
his eyes and looked brazenly right into Derek's. It
was Derek who lowered his.

"Oh?" said Derek. "I didn't know you had one.
Sigourney, what did you do today?"

What did I do today? I bought a sophisticated
cocktail dress, black! I didn't answer the silly question at all.

Peter wandered to the door. "I'll be here for the
party," he said, a slight sneer on his pretty mouth.
"Marie told me last night, you didn't forget to ask
me, did you?"

(Marie!)

"Just a few friends to meet my wife," said Derek.
"You are always welcome."

"What shall I wear?" asked Peter, kicking at the
carpet.

"If I were you," said Derek, "you look best in . . ."

and he stopped. I was perfectly amazed at two men discussing what they would wear. I longed to say, "How about a black cocktail dress, black is so smart."

"I spent the last of my allowance on those pink shirts you wanted me to have," said Peter.

Derek drew out his billfold and flipped Peter some new bills without counting them.

"A slight loan," he said, "until the fifteenth."

Peter did not even thank him.

"Derek," I said as soon as the door closed, "who is Marie?"

"Marie?" He seemed to think I was going to ask him something else.

"Yes, Marie, Peter said Marie told him about the party." Why was Derek playing so stupid?

"Marie is Peter's mother."

"She *is?*"

"Yes. You will meet her tomorrow."

"How old is she?"

"You must learn not to ask how old people are," said Derek.

"Why?"

"It's very unsophisticated," said Derek.

"Hmmm," I said sarcastically, "how interesting."

"Marie is a woman of no age," said Derek. "She is a very beautiful and intelligent woman, that's all."

"And what about me!" I was furious. "What about me!"

Derek took me by the nape of the neck. "You are an adorable child," he said, "a naughty boy."

"I'm a woman!" I cried and I longed to be. I longed to be a beautiful and intelligent woman, ageless.

Derek just like Peter a minute ago plopped me face down on the couch.

"Can't you love me right side up!" I yelled and I beat the pillow with my fists.

Derek disappeared into the kitchen. I sat up on the couch and looked into space, a clear space with nothing in it at all, just like Derek I stared into nothing. I didn't think anything or see anything or feel anything. I suppose it was restful. Then I heard Derek moving around in the kitchen. I heard the icebox door open and close and the egg beater whirring in a china bowl. He came in and reached for the telephone without noticing me. He called the liquor store on the corner. He discussed several wines, he was enjoying himself immensely, he insisted at first on Batard Montrachet, a white Burgundy 1959 (Pouilly Fuisse), but then he considered Chablis les clos, Grand Cru also 1959 or possibly Corton Charlemagne. He and the liquor man discussed the year, the town, the vintage, the "stature" of the wine, it must be estate bottled. At last Derek said, "Yes, yes, that will be perfect, just right, thank you." He hung up.

"How talented you are," I said.

"Talented?"

"All that jazz about vintage," I said, "and stature and estate bottled, cripes."

" 'Jazz'? Where did you pick that up?" he said.

"In the slums!" I yelled. "And I don't want a soufflé, I don't want a Chablis les clos or a Montrachet. Can't we have fricasseed chicken and Brown Betty and a tumbler of hard cider?"

"For goodness sake!" said Derek.

"Aren't you ever just plain hungry? Aren't you ever thirsty?"

"One doesn't drink a Chablis les clos 1959 at six-fifty when one is thirsty," said Derek.

"That's what I *mean!*" I cried. "I'm tired," I sobbed. "I can't have fricasseed chicken when I'm hungry, I can't have a tumbler of cider when I'm thirsty, what can I do when I'm tired! I don't suppose it would be sophisticated to lie down and go to sleep."

The kitchen doorbell rang, it was the man with the wine and I calmed down for propriety's sake, besides, I didn't have anything more to say. As the door swung open I smelled the sweetness and the brownness of the soufflé. It did smell delicious. Derek came back patting the precious bottle of wine, estate bottled, price six-fifty.

"I know you will like it," he said. "Sigourney," he

said, "shall I just run out and get a quarter of a pound of caviar?"

"What in God's name are we celebrating!" I cried. "Oh, all right."

" 'Oh, all right,' she says," said Derek. "You *are* spoiled! Don't touch the oven door, don't even walk around in the kitchen and don't let Sydney bark, the soufflé mustn't fall." And he left.

I can't even go out in my own kitchen, I said to myself. Sydney sat up in her chair and yawned.

"Sydney! Look out for the soufflé!" I giggled.

Well, maybe I am spoiled, the supper was delicious, the wine went to my head and made my eyes shine and Derek was sweet to me—"A little more, Sigourney, it won't hurt you."

"I wish it would," I said. "I've been hateful, I'm sorry, Derek, let me wash the dishes."

"Oh, I love doing the dishes," said Derek.

"But Derek, let's just not do the dishes at all, wouldn't that be fun?"

I wanted him to make love to me.

"It won't take a minute," said Derek.

"But Derek . . ."

"You're tired, Sigourney, from that fitting, go along to bed and I'll do the dishes and then I ought to run over to Mother's for a little while."

"Oh."

"I'll try not to wake you when I come in."

And he didn't.

"You leave me alone and I'll leave you alone, you leave me alone and I'll leave you alone," *Oh bury me not on the lone prairie* and the something or other, something or other, something or other . . . That's how I fell asleep, waiting in vain for Derek.

Oh Sydney, Sydney, where is our girlhood?

8

"Did you enjoy the party, Sigourney?"

"Yes," I said shortly.

"I was proud of you but . . ."

"But what? The hell with thith thipper."

Derek laughed. "You'll have to learn to hold your liquor. Here, let me do it," and he unzipped my sophisticated cocktail dress that had wowed the guests at the party.

"I wowed them," I said, I kicked off the very high heels, "didn't I? I wowed them bug-eyed."

"Really," said Derek.

"Rally," I mimicked him.

"Don't be disagreeable," said Derek.

"I'm pooped," I said, "I'm pooped beyond compare. Who zat?"

"Where?"

"In the meer."

All of a sudden I said in a high voice, "Petah! Petah! Petah!"

"Stop it!" said Derek.

"Oh Petah this, and Petah that, and my deah you're the image of Petah. You didn't disguise me at all in that stupid old cocktail dress. Here!" I picked up the divine black dress and threw it at Derek. "Give it to Petah!" I cried, inspired.

Derek's silence was awesome. I was frightened but I said, "That little fairy!" I was way ahead of myself, what was I talking about . . .

Slap! Derek struck me so hard my head spun round and round.

"Little beast!" he said.

"What what what!" I said, and I felt the softness of Peter's cheek that had so infuriated me that I struck him again.

Derek slapped me again. I was getting used to it but as he came toward me once more, I straight-armed him and lifted my leg, I kicked him around behind, it was easy, my stockinged toe got him between the buttocks.

Oh what a row! I thought. We're having a real row!

"You too!" I cried. "You too!"

"Me too?" He gripped me by the shoulders.

"You too," I said weakly and I started to cry, I never last long.

"Come to bed," said Derek.

"No no no! Not that!"

He lifted me easily and carried me into the bedroom. This is not so bad, I thought, this is all right.

Well, he did it. He wasn't gentle, he just did it, and when he was finished he stood up and looked at my helpless body (I thought, I don't look much with my slip around my neck and my sheer black stockings around my ankles) and then as he stood there he gave my legs a shove. Why? What was he thinking? It was a gesture I remember of Daddy's after Sunday dinner when he'd had enough. It was almost a gesture of disgust. There would be only a little mashed potato and gravy left on the plate and he'd shove it away. Mama didn't like it, you could tell by the way she lifted her eyebrows and narrowed her nose, but Daddy was just a male, his table manners weren't very good. He was a bad example.

Derek went into the bathroom and I pulled the quilt up over myself and didn't say anything, I guess I had said enough. I was sober again. I had felt no pleasure at all when he did it. To hell with it.

I lay there. Derek came out of the bathroom. He had had the last word, I suppose, as usual, if that is what you could call it, and I had lost. He looked as

impeccably dressed as usual down to the shining
pointed shoes. "I think I'll just take a turn in the
park," he said.

"Look out," I said.

"What?"

"Don't sit down," I said, "in the park."

He left. I wanted to cry out, "Derek come back,"
but I didn't have the energy, besides it wouldn't
mean a thing. The door opened and closed. I felt the
slight chill I always feel when a door closes. There
seems to me to be always a finality about that click.

I'm not a bit tired, I might as well write about the
party although it's hardly worth it. Except for Marie
and the bums. The little apartment on stilts is spin-
nings and I am in the very center of it like something
in a bottle. Centrifugal force I think it's called, it is
quite pleasant.

Derek's sister Louise doesn't look like Derek at all,
except for her ears and the way she walks. Sliding
up to me, she kissed me and said, "My dear," turned
her back, which is rather elegant, and glided over to
the bar and poured herself a whisky and soda. In
spite of the split-second perusal she had given me, I
felt she had taken me in all right, not just my stylish
clothes, she knew all about me. I imagine she was
surprised, though, to see me looking so chic, I even
had some eyeshadow on at Derek's suggestion. Another woman came in with Louise but Louise hardly

spoke to her all evening except to call her Blessèd twice. She looked far from "blessèd," she looked as if she had been crying for two years, but she wore a smart suit, the color of an eggplant, aubergine Derek described it, and her hair fell over her forehead rather rakishly as if once maybe long ago when she was fourteen she'd been a real problem to her parents for some reason or other. Unlike Louise, she stared at me a long time before she, too, turned her back and helped herself to a big drink, straight. All during the party I felt her eyes on me.

Peter came in looking like a rose and with him three young men, none of them any older than I, and all of them made for the bar without a word.

"Who are *they*?" I said to Derek.

"Bums! I didn't invite them!" said Derek, and I was startled.

"Bums?" I whispered.

"Ssssh," said Derek. "Marie!"

"Dear boy," said Marie.

"This is my wife."

"Ahhh," said Marie.

"Sigourney," said Derek.

"Sigourney," said Marie. "What a charming name, and she's the image of Petah."

"I don't think so," said Derek, I thought rather bluntly for him, usually so suave.

"I'm in disguise," I said, I felt immediately at ease

with the beautiful ageless one. She looked at me inquiringly.

"In my smart cocktail dress," I said, "I just bought
it yesterday or rather Derek did, and my black stockings."

"They're exquisite," said Marie, "so smart."

"And my high heels, I feel dizzy in them." I
laughed, "Eeek."

"But why are you in disguise?" Marie smiled.

"Because I really look like a boy," I said, "and
Derek didn't think I should come to the party looking like a boy, so he took me to Bergdorf's and it was
a scream, the saleslady almost made him buy me
some enormous . . ." I stopped because Marie wore
two strands of enormous . . .

I saw Marie glance at Derek. She was amused and
keen.

"Dear boy," she said, laughing, a tender little
laugh, a sweet gurgle, "Pygmalion, how it suits you."

I looked at Derek, he was very pale, a sudden
silence had come over the room, it was like Derek's
own silence. It was a combination of one of Derek's
silences and the beautiful intelligent woman's ability to stop traffic and time in its tracks, even the delivery boy on the bicycle. Like a still in the middle
of a movie, everyone at the bar turned and looked
into the camera and even I stood immobile.

Then Louise laughed, a harsh laugh, almost a mean laugh; the cameras started grinding again.

I remembered my manners and offered a tray of hors d'oeuvres, but I was frightened, something had happened, why had Derek frozen like that? Why had he turned pale? Was he ill?

"These are good," I said, putting my forefinger on the tiny crescents of shrimp. "Try one of these."

"They're simply divine," said Marie, taking three and popping them into her mouth.

I passed them to the bums. "Thanks," said the bums and didn't take any. Their faces were flushed from the liquor. I smiled at them, they were young like me, but they looked at me with contempt, at my smart cocktail dress, my sheer black stockings, my high heels. "Peter," I said gaily, "you aren't much help," and I shoved the tray of hors d'oeuvres toward him, "pass these."

Peter reached out his arm and I saw the bracelet well up on his wrist. "What's that?" I almost said but something stopped me. Not the bums, however. "How adorable!" they all said in unison. Funny language for bums, I thought.

Several more guests arrived and Derek introduced me. I don't know who they were, Marie kept coming to my assistance because I had nothing to say to them and after their first *My dear*'s and *How d'ya do*'s, they simply stared at me and looked bored to death. Even the powerful highballs didn't cheer them up or change their look of detachment and indifference. I decided it was smart to look dull and that I would try it sometime.

Louise's friend sat against the wall in a straight chair, her legs stretched way out, and drank highball after highball that somebody was supplying her with and didn't say anything and nobody spoke to her. They stepped over her as if she were an empty crate on the sidewalk. Gradually a simple smile spread over her face and she looked almost pretty, girlish. "Blessèd!" I heard Louise say, but Blessèd didn't seem to hear and Louise couldn't be seen, not from where I stood anyway. A little later I heard it again —"Blessèd!" and Blessèd looked up at the ceiling and for all I know that's where Louise was.

What a stupid party, I said to myself and I up-ended my own glass, maybe it would help.

"It's a pretty awful party," said Marie in my ear as if she were saying something else like, "The hors d'oeuvres are delicious," "but you'll get used to them."

"You mean there's going to be another!" I shouted but no one heard me, I might as well have been in the middle of Times Square.

Then Peter began horsing around with the bums.

*"Matelot, Matelot, Where you go, My heart goes
with you!"*—one of the bums had the look of a sailor
—*"When you go down to the sea."* Another had very
long lashes and dark holes in his cheeks as if he
never slept and when he looked in my direction once,
he looked as if he were facing a strong light, the
pupils of his eyes no bigger than the head of a pin,
the third was very good-looking, almost as pretty as
Peter and it was that one that Peter chose to tease.
They all began shoving each other around and cuf-
fing each other and roughhousing like a lot of kids
and I longed to join them. Soon they were an in-
extricable mass, you wouldn't know who was who or
which legs belonged to whom, but I saw Peter free
himself from the grip of the sailor, who had him
around the thighs, and falling forward off balance
he grabbed the handsome one and bit his neck quick.

"You little bitch!" cried the handsome one.

It came out clear as a message on a valentine
above the scuffling and the laughter, the clatter of
ice in glasses, the loud voices of the other guests, you
couldn't miss it, it was so clean-cut and shocking, it
had a special timbre, when I was little I had a toy
bulldog in a tiny house and if you said "Come out!"
in a special tone, it did. I deliberately closed my
mouth because it hung open and looked across the
room at Derek. There was a look of private outrage

on his handsome knifelike face, a kind of dangerous
fury. The bums extricated themselves, adjusted their
clothes and made for the bar. They were a flushed
and disorderly lot but they shone like angels. What
fun! Except for Derek the others paid little attention
to the rumpus, simply holding their highballs high
so they wouldn't be spilled and talking away like
mad. I saw Marie go up to Derek and take his arm,
but the gesture was more like a groom quieting a
skittish mare. I expected to see Derek rear and paw
the air, what was the matter with him?

Then I saw Peter stand aside from the others and
stare at Derek as if no one else were present; on his
charming face also a look of that same private outrage, followed almost at once by his usual deep sulk.
I tried to catch his eye to smile at him to let him
know that I didn't mind the disturbance, that I
thought it was fun. How we all used to roughhouse
in the country on a rainy day, I and my cousins and
the neighbors' boys, a kind of bodily kinship, but I
felt someone else looking at me, it was Blessèd and
I smiled at her instead. Her big eyes looking out from
under her dark fringe of hair looked like a basset
hound's. She was very drunk. No one spoke to her,
she might as well have been in a hole in the ground.
Louise was still laughing a kind of nervous mean
laugh, a running commentary, a voluble sneer, it

seemed, it had a cutting edge and everyone was meant to feel it, but if anyone was cut by it, no one showed his scars. These people are real tough, I said to myself. Do they were bulletproof vests, maybe Warner Brothers trims them with nylon lace, and for the gentlemen cummerbunds by DuPont. Someone gave me a drink; I felt a hand on my leg but I didn't see anybody.

"Sigourney, what a lovely name. My dear child, you look just like Peter. She's the image of Peter."

I looked around; I was bored now that the bums were orderly again. I could only see the solid phalanx of their backs as they faced the bar, nothing but their buttocks, I thought, to see. I looked around at the smartly dressed women and the equally smartly dressed men. I looked and listened. They were all talking away but no one made a gesture, their lips did not seem to move, the sound of their voices might have been coming out of their ears, their faces remained expressionless and the women's voices sounded like the men's, there was no inflection. Maybe they all had artificial larynxes. I listened. Phrases and single words detached themselves from the well-bred roar as of a train coming into Windsor Locks on Sunday:

". . . It was fabulous, my dear, simply fabulous. I never watch television. Majorca, Florence, Indone-

sia. Silk. The biggest emerald. Is she like that? My
dear, it's unbelievable. Who do you think it was?
No! I'm positive. With all that money you'd think.
It's a standard poodle. What's the matter with her?
Silver. It's the tourists. But the other one is by far.
De Gaulle. Not exactly. Perhaps I shouldn't say so.
My dear, who has time for a cup of tea. She's sweet
but. I ought to run along. Do you suppose there's a
john in this apartment. She's very pretty, I'm surprised. It's very unusual, they usually prefer older
women. Peter. You would think Marie. I think she
comes from Connecticut. Really? I think I'll have a
gin and tonic. Marie darling! Crème brûlée. Oh it's
easy. I told my cook. Gin and tonic. No thanks, old
man. The market closed at. What do you expect.
I.B.M. It's perfectly ridiculous. It's much too small.
She told me so herself. I think it's between Park and
Madison. Good heavens no! I really couldn't care
less. She took off twenty pounds. She looks a sight.
But that isn't exactly what I mean. I haven't an idea.
It's not my affair. Paris, oh Paris. He shot himself
you know. Oh yes, he certainly did. My dear, what
does it matter. I was thrilled to death. Did you see
it? I've seen it four times. Off Broadway. Oh Holly-
wood, my dear. If you ask me, old man, I think it
stinks. Good*night*, I said and I meant it. Don't bother
to buy it, I'll lend it to you. It's awfully sexy. I think

it's a copy, Balenciaga. Frightful taste. My dear,
they're all that way. It makes me sick, I thought I'd
vomit. They're at all the parties now. Don't be so
naïve, Maude. My dear, the zipper broke, I thought
I'd have to go to bed in it. It was screamingly funny.
I decided to tie one on and I did. He's a decorator.
Imagine it. Why, of course, what do you think?
Thanks old man, not right now. Complete hysterec-
tomy. No wonder. You're kidding. Metrecal. Swed-
ish. A little woman who gives a heavenly massage.
Flamenco. That isn't what I said. Nobody goes there
any more. It just takes guts. That isn't the way I
heard it. How absurd! You mean she told you that
herself, my dear? Well I heard it differently. How
loathsome! *Swan Lake.* He's what you call a pillar
of the church and he has the Legion of Honor. It
was a lovely concert. I adore Beethoven. Which one,
my dear? Bach. Wrong side of the tracks. *Noblesse
oblige.* Thanks old man. Coricidin. She's a white Russian. I had to, what else could I do? Idlewild. Here,
use my lighter. What possible difference does it
make. You simply stick it in the oven. He's a real
gourmet. Remind me to tell you . . ."

The exclamation points are mine, likewise the
semicolons and commas. It all ran together and the
tone was flat, there was a complete lack of enthusiasm. A couple of older men had joined the bums and

Peter at the bar. Thank God the party is over, some
invisible gong must have gone off because all of a
sudden everyone is gone, there was a crush at the
door; all of a sudden everybody just had to be somewhere else—"My dear, I'm due at Maggie's an hour
ago."

Derek alone stood by the window staring out, motionless. I went to the little powder room, I had to,
and there sitting on the john was the last guest,
Blessèd.

"Excuse me," I said.

"Where's Weezie?" She was in tears, big tears
rolled down her cheeks, her eyes were drowned in
them.

"Who?"

"Weezie, Weezie," she sobbed.

"Weezie?" I suddenly realized she meant Louise
and I almost laughed, the elegant Louise: Weezie!
It was a metamorphosis I couldn't handle in my
brain. "You mean Louise?"

"Weezie left Blessèd all alone."

"Come, I'll help you," I said. "I'll get you a cab.
Whoops! You're all right."

"Bye now."

"Bye."

"You're sweet," said Blessèd.

I couldn't get rid of her.

"Sydney," I called, I whistled. "Sydney, you can come out now."

Blessèd looked startled.

Sydney came out of the kitchen looking exhausted and irritable.

"Good dog!" I said.

"I got to go," said Blessèd. "You're sweet," she said. "I hate Weezie."

"Oh no," I said. I didn't care.

"Yeth," she lisped. "She's a bitch." She said it with wide-open eyes as if she had broken a dish.

The door swung open and in walked Louise, immaculate and elegant. "Come on," she said to Blessèd.

"Dearest," sobbed Blessèd. "Weezie."

Louise laughed. "What a sight you are. You'll have to excuse her," she said to me. "Dolores is an original."

"Oh," I said stupidly. She looked more like a wet doll with a broken face, I thought, dressed up in Mama's best suit—Aubergine, said Derek.

"Blessèd," said Louise sternly, "stop crying and come along, say good-by."

"Bye now," said Blessèd contentedly.

"Sydney, what a day!"

Ghastly, said Sydney.

9

But the day wasn't over. Sydney and I went out into
the park where Derek had gone for a turn. I knew
better, I learn fast, than to go after him but by
chance perhaps . . . well, there he was and there was
Marie! They were walking toward us arm in arm.
They looked so stunningly handsome together I
wanted to stare as if they were strangers from another country, but I felt a terrible stabbing jealousy
and I looked like a country lout. I had on my going-
away suit that only two weeks ago was so smart, I
thought, but now it might have been a Mother Hub-
bard or a sack. "A sack!" I said out loud and Sydney
waved her tail in response, and seeing Derek,
strained at her leash to let me know it was he. The
little boy who had first asked me what kind of a dog
she was, skipped by with his mother and sing-

songed, "It's the hound dog, it's the hound dog, it's the houuund dawg." "Come!" said his mother, shaking his arm, "don't stare." Again it was as if Marie were in slow motion because of the intensity of my gaze, all the details I was taking in; again everything else slowed down, even the little boy. Not only were they arm in arm but Derek was clasping her wrist. Why, they looked like lovers! Oblivious to everything, everyone, time, place! Marie was too sophisticated and Derek too stuffy to hold hands in the park, Derek always treated me like an acquaintance in public, he is very aware of the public. But there they were coming toward me, so intent on each other that I need not turn and run, I don't exist. I leashed in Sydney, she seemed to understand, and they passed us by. My eyes were full of tears and when the big park policeman touched his cap at Sydney and me, I wanted to throw myself into his arms. Daddy! As they passed I heard Marie say ". . . Dear boy . . ." Dear boy! I snarled inwardly. The rat!

Sydney sat down hard. She was tired and wanted to go home. I turned and there they were ahead of me. Marie, I thought, of course Marie, Marie is his woman, his equal. They moved along so closely that their thighs were rubbing together at each step. Marie managed her high heels so cleverly that she might have been barefoot. At the length of Derek's

free arm the hateful Homburg hung and Marie wore
no hat at all. Their profiles as each turned and looked
into the eyes of the other were so close that . . . they
were kissing! It can't be possible! but the kiss lasted.
Marie swayed a little, and Derek guided her to the
park bench. I stopped. Were they going to neck on
a park bench! They were. Where was the nice policeman? But the clever Marie seemed to have cre-
ated a kind of peaceful vacuum around her and her
lover. There wasn't anyone in sight, a kind of haze
settled in, almost a fog, as the air grew chill like in
November, but the moisture in the air carried their
voices to me as if they were at sea. "Do you love me?"
Marie's voice was achingly tender, the stupid question, the question of an inexperienced girl, me! lost
its banality and Derek's sickening reply attracted
and repelled me; a sexual disgust raised the hairs on
the back of my neck. Sydney was waiting patiently,
her tongue hanging out. The lights came on in the
park, around each lamp a shining ring like around
the moon. "Baby," I heard Derek say. "Never leave
me," said Marie. So the International Set has as limited a love vocabulary as the others, I said to myself.
They stood up. Derek's hand was on Marie's sleek
thigh. Marie stretched and sighed as if she were in
her own room. Suddenly they took off, there was no
more conversation, if that's what you can call a mon-

osyllabic discourse such as theirs. They walked fast,
they disappeared in the fog. I visualized a plump
hand pulling down the shade, a wedding band on
one of the fingers, but that was the thirty-five-year-
old woman when Derek was . . . On the bench, all
out of proportion in the queer light, suspended like
a rowboat on a lake, was Derek's hateful Homburg,
gigantic. What did it mean? It means something,
that black blob, forgotten on the park bench, that
precious Homburg that Derek tends as carefully as
if it were part of his body.

Sydney raised herself on her hind legs and sniffed
the thing as if it were another dog, to find out what
it was thinking, I suppose, was it a friend or an en-
emy? She gave a joyful yip, a friend. "Derek hates
you," I said to her. "He can't stand you," but she
nuzzled the Homburg as she nuzzles Derek between
the legs. How it annoys him! "But she doesn't know
it isn't the thing to do," I say. I picked it up, it would
be indecent to leave it there for all the world to see.

I put the Homburg in the closet on the top shelf
and shut the door.

I snapped on all the lights in the apartment. How
silent it was, even the traffic outside muted by the
fog. I could hear the toilet dribbling. Blessèd must
have been rough with it. I fixed it. The rosy carpet,

wall to wall, was badly trampled from all the feet of
the guests at the party, the ladies' spike heels had
made tiny, deep, circular indentations and the gentlemen's pointed footprints were clearly visible.
There must be well-defined fingerprints on all the
glasses, too, not to mention lipstick smears, a variety
of colors. For some reason I said, "A bunch of ban-
dits and their molls."

Honey Honey Honey Honey, that tune, I am beginning to hate it, *There's Honey on the Moon Tonight. . . . Come along and let's taste it . . . It's a pity
to waste it with a honey like you.* Marie! Marie and
Derek! I put my hands over my eyes to try to make
disappear their disappearance into the pinkish fog,
the plump hand of the wrong woman pulling down
the shade. A case of mistaken identity. A little girl is
passing by in her perambulator. It is I, too young
to be a witness in any court.

The telephone rang.

I let it ring. It rang and rang, angrily I thought,
but I sat on the couch and let it ring. How sad, I
thought, there's a girl sitting on the couch in an
empty room and the telephone is ringing and she
doesn't answer it. Does she hear it? It was more like
a picture of a telephone ringing than a telephone
really ringing. Probably there were little wavy lines
around the bell, sound waves, but they didn't reach

the girl's ears and that's why she didn't answer the
picture of the telephone.

Sigourney. The girl looked up, the telephone
stopped ringing. Sigourney. Yes, the girl said, what?
Why didn't you answer the telephone? I didn't hear
it. Yes you did. I didn't want to answer it. Why?
Why should I? It's customary. What would I say if
I answered it? The usual thing. I am trying to think.
Why don't you get out of here? Why don't you run
away? Oh yes, said the girl out loud, I ran away
twice when I was little but I never left my room.
Besides there's nothing to run away from, you only
run away from home and this isn't home, I have no
home.

At this sad speech someone was crying. Idiot! I
said. The toilet was dribbling again. Dolores is an
original, Louise said.

Why don't you kill him?

She raised the gun and pulled the trigger. Click!
The gun didn't go off, it sounded like the front door.

"Sigourney, why are you sitting there in the dark?"
said Derek.

He stood quietly in front of me, my handsome
Derek, from his left arm, long like a monkey's, dan-
gled the hateful Homburg. I stared at it.

"I'm not sitting in the dark," I said. "All the lights
are on." But they weren't, the only light in the room

came in the windows from the city. I distinctly remembered snapping the switch that lights up the
whole apartment when I came in.

"You snapped the lights off when you came in," I
said, "instead of on."

"Possibly," said Derek.

"Why are you holding your hat in your hand?" I
said. "You usually put it in the closet." I jumped up
and ran to the hall, snapped on the lights and looked
into the closet.

"It's not there," I said. "You must have left it in
the park. On a bench," I added.

"I have it in my hand," said Derek. "Aren't you a
little confused?"

"Oh no," I said, "I'm not a bit confused, it's you
who are confused."

"Let's not quarrel," said Derek gently. He put the
Homburg on the shelf and shut the closet door.

"Lock it!" I said excitedly.

"Why?" he said.

"It might get out! I hate it!" I said. "I hate your
hateful Homburg!"

"Come off it," said Derek impatiently.

"Marie!" I cried.

"Marie?" said Derek, cold as ice.

"Derek!" I cried. "Don't ever leave me!" I meant it.

"Baby," he said, he repeated it, "Baby," and he

put his arms around me. I almost succumbed, but then I heard the limited love talk like a recording in my brain—"Don't ever leave me," said Marie. "Baby," said Derek.

"Peter!" I said, stamping my foot, I was talking wildly, I have no idea why I dragged in Peter.

"Peter?" said Derek, raising his eyebrows.

"Peter, yes," I said, "he called you a minute ago."

The telephone rang. Neither the man nor the girl moved.

"Answer it," said the girl.

"Let it ring," said the man.

It rang and rang, the picture of the telephone like an ad in a magazine, Have you called your loved ones lately?

The man held the girl's hand so tightly it hurt.

"Why don't you answer it?" she said.

"There's no need to," he said.

The telephone stopped.

"Did you enjoy the party?" Derek said.

"But we've been through all that," I said.

"What?"

"Don't you remember," I said, "we had a hell of a row . . . then . . . Didn't we?" I said doubtfully. "And then you . . ."

He said nothing.

"And then you . . ." I said, "did it to me." I blushed.

It was the first time either of us had mentioned the unspeakable . . . the act.

"You have a very limited vocabulary," Derek said.

"You fucked me," I said loud and clear. I was horrified at what I said. It was Allyn who taught me the word I thought I had forgotten, but that's what the girl said.

The lights in Derek's eyes were like the two pilot lights in the gas stove. Frightened to death, I waited for that special silence, the terrible withdrawal. I can't think what the girl looked like standing there, possibly on tiptoe, ready to take off, with that dirty word in her still open mouth. Did she look like some kind of challenge, a boxer, or what did she look like? But the man didn't withdraw into his special silence as was expected at all, he became strangely animated and much sooner than these lines could have been written, he said:

"Faggot." And then as if he were thinking it over to be sure, he repeated it, "Faggot," very thoughtfully.

It must be a dirty word, a word that children in the International Set use, I had said one so Derek said one, too. I felt more at ease. "Shit," I said.

Derek grabbed my arms. "Naughty boy," he said tenderly, oh so tenderly. He slid his strong long arms

down the length of me and then he spun me around,
I was still on my toes, like a top.

"No!" I yelled, weakened by the tenderness in his
voice, fighting it desperately. "Leave me alone! Why
. . ." I stuttered, "why . . . you don't even know who
I am."

He let go. "Who are you?" he said coldly.

"Me!" I said, thumping the girl's chest, "I!" spreading my fingers on my shoulders. "Sigourney!"

"Very dramatic," said Derek.

The girl raised the gun. No, wait.

"You have taken away my identity," I said.

"Quite profound," said Derek.

"Shut up!" I cried. "Murderer!"

"Come come," said Derek, bored. "I think I'll go
over to Mother's."

"To whose!" I screamed.

Derek turned calmly at the door. "Take an aspirin
and go to bed, you're overtired."

"I'm not a prostitute," I sobbed. Oh Derek Derek
Derek (to myself), *Honey Honey Honey, There's
Honey on the Moon Tonight* (to myself). The door
closed gently in my face. Click.

She's crazy, I said and I went aimlessly, rudder-
less, into the kitchenette, maybe she was hungry.
She took a Coke out of the icebox, flipped off the top
that spun under the table and sucked at the cold

bottle, trying to warm it with her mouth. Not until
she had finished it did she realize she was thirsty.
She ate all the little hors d'oeuvres that were left
from the party and rinsed off the plate, no, she licked
the plate, it was pleasanter. I wasn't thinking about
anything, just watching the girl. Then I saw the mail
that had been pushed under the door, a few scattered
letters, maybe bills, I looked at a post card with
pleasure: Capri. The blue grotto with a pink rowboat. *It's simply divine here. J.* It was addressed to
Derek. I looked at another card: *You will be receiv-
ing a free sample of Fabulosa soon.* It was simply addressed: *Occupant.*

So! A premonition of some sort! I was right. I had
lost my identity. Derek had taken away the girl's
identity. Arson! Manslaughter! Rape!

I'll put it in Derek's bureau drawer, I said to myself, and he'll find it and I just won't explain. I'll say,
"Oh, it must be for me, that's the way all my mail is
addressed."

The telephone rang.

I paid no attention. No one paid any attention. I
opened the top drawer and slid the card under the
bracelet.

What bracelet!

There it was, the pretty bracelet I had seen before.
I lifted it out. How pretty it was, a silver band of

turquoises. Darling Derek, he has brought me a present, I mustn't let him know I have seen it, I will put the card somewhere else. But it is the bracelet I saw on Peter! The very same—"How adorable!" the bums cried. I slipped the bracelet on my wrist and pushed it up where Peter's had been on his, I saw the fine hairs on the back of Peter's long hand. "How adorable!" cried the bums. I put the bracelet carefully back. Perhaps he forgot to give it to me for the party, but no, it would not go with the black cocktail dress at all, Derek certainly knew that, only spare chalk-white cultured pearls . . . two strands like . . .

The telephone rang.

I ran to it. "Hello!" I said. "There's nobody here," and I hung up. I felt much better, as if I had won at tennis.

The door opened and Derek came in. He handed me the long-stemmed yellow roses.

"There now," he said as if to a child. "I didn't go to Mother's, I came back to get you a little supper and put you to bed."

"Oh, I've eaten," I said. "I licked the plate. Thank you, Derek darling, how beautiful they are." There were tears in my eyes again but I didn't let Derek see them as I put the roses in the green vase and stood back to admire them, they looked very lovely, impressionistic, and they shivered because of the tears.

It's the only way to look at roses, I decided, making a
note in my brain that was full of odds and ends.

And where were you, Sydney, during all of the
above, my only friend who loves me for myself and
doesn't care about all that sort of thing. Oh you
know, bracelets, illicit kisses, spike heels; the dirty
word came into my mind and Sydney looked up. Oh
yes, that she knows about. It's onomatopoeic. And
speaking of odds and ends, what about the sentence
I overheard out of all the gabble at the party: "They
usually prefer older women." You leave me alone
and I'll leave you alone, said Derek. I hear the mirth-
less laugh of Louise.

"Derek?"

"Yes."

"Who's your mother?"

Derek didn't answer but he put down the cookbook; "Marie," he said, "likes beef kidneys, go to
the butcher tomorrow and get . . ." he picked up the
cookbook again ". . . a pound, I imagine they weigh
about that."

"Eeeek," I said.

"You must learn to like different things and
sauces," said Derek. "Your taste in food is very limited. George Meredith said you could tell a gentleman by his acquired tastes."

"And how can you tell a lady?" I said sarcastically.

"The same is true of a lady," said Derek solemnly. "Now go to bed, I'm tired."

"*Me* go to bed because *you're* tired," I said. "I hope you didn't sit down in the park!" I added suddenly. I was on dangerous ground but I felt like a child who wants to astonish his mother even if, and perhaps because, he gets licked for it. I didn't dare accuse him of going home with, at least into the fog with, Marie; he might kill me.

"How many Homburgs have you got!" I cried.

"You won't forget the kidney?" said Derek.

I gave up, he couldn't be roused.

We lay side by side in the dark without moving or touching, at least I suppose so. For all I knew, Derek could have been sleeping with Marie or making a soufflé. I went sound asleep. I'd make a lousy witness. What did he wear? Nothing. What did he say? Nothing. The witness may step down. Exhausted, confused, I stepped down into oblivion, I didn't dream anything at all.

So I went to the butcher's, little sucker that I am, to please Derek so he could please Marie.

"I want a beef kidney, I imagine they weigh about a pound," I said to the butcher with the bloody

apron. He disappeared into the big icebox. Click. It
must be cold in there.

"And this is my honeymoon," I said out loud. "To
hell with it!"

The butcher reappeared with an enormous hunk
of fat. He lugged it out and plunked it down on the
wooden table that had a big scoop in it from all the
beheadings and atrocities and autopsies, maybe hys-
terectomies.

"Is that a beef kidney?" I asked, astonished.

"It's inside, miss."

"Oh."

With a flashing big knife he cut into the big hunk
of fat at just the right place and the fat fell away
disclosing a thing: black.

"How did you know it was there?" I said admiringly.

The butcher smiled conceitedly. He brandished
the knife and made a second and a third incision,
freeing the thing from the fat entirely. It rolled onto
the table, sodden and inert. With a lewd grin he
cupped it in his big-knuckled red hand, seeming to
weigh it, he raised his eyes skyward. "A pound," he
said, as he dumped it on the scale. "Righto." The
kidney slumped, motionless, it looked like Derek's
Homburg on the park bench.

I laughed.

The butcher raised his eyebrows.

"It looks like my husband's Homburg," I explained.

"It sure do," said the butcher, he winked at me.

I blushed. "Please wrap it up good," I said. "I mean, put it in two bags." I had a horror of the bulky wet thing that seemed to be adjusting itself in the cup of the butcher's big hand, was it still alive? How disgusting it was. Marie can have it! I said to myself on the way home. She's going to eat it! Derek and Marie are going to eat the thing! I shuddered. A ritual, I said, a ritual of some sort, a fertility rite. Eeeek. Whoops! The brakes screeched.

"Look where you're goin'!" yelled the furious taxi driver. I stepped back onto the curb.

"Want to get killed," said the cop threateningly.

"Yes," I said.

"Wait for the light," he said.

"Okay," I said sulkily.

He looked at my legs. "All right now," he said, "the light's changed. Take it easy, miss."

He doesn't believe me, I said, that I want to get killed, he doesn't know how unhappy I am, look at me on my honeymoon carrying an amoeba or something disgusting in a paper bag for *them* to eat. It could be somebody's head, I'll throw it in the trash can there, I can't stand it any longer. There was a

spot of blood on the bag already, the thing was seep-
ing through. In a panic—You're crazy, said the girl,
All right, all right, I *am*, I said, I lifted up the top
of the container and dumped the beastly thing in,
plunk! Before I did it I looked both ways but no one
was looking, the law was sauntering away, swinging
his club around his wrist. A man on a bench was
buried to his shoulders in his newspaper. A priest,
his big feet kicking forward his skirts as he walked,
was telling his beads. I was invisible, anonymous, an
occupant, nobody. I almost ran the rest of the way
home, feeling guilty but relieved and planning a lie,
a good one. At least I had rid myself of the soggy
evidence. Derek darling, they didn't have any beef
kidneys, they're out of season. No, he would know
better, beef are never out of season, but maybe their
kidneys taste funny this time of year. The butcher
said the kidneys are all dried up this time of year.
I was nearly home, I slowed down. Someone came
up behind me and grabbed the bag and ran like hell.
No No! I yelled. Come back here! But the boy, he
wore a plaid shirt and jeans and his hair was brown
and kind of kinky, disappeared in the crowd. Crowd?
I looked around, nobody. The boy disappeared
around the big building on the corner. What do you
suppose he wanted with an old dried-up kidney?
The boy opened the bag and looked in, Ugh! he

threw the whole bag away, it landed with a plop on the sidewalk and a stray dog sniffed at it but even he didn't want it. A big slinky alley cat darted out of nowhere and grabbed the kidney out of the bag and loped off, her tail high to balance the weight of the kidney, it weighed a pound. You dumped the kidney in the trash container, said the girl. Hell, I know it, I said, and I'm glad of it.

"I'm not a pimp!" I said to Derek.

"What are you talking about?" said Derek. "Where do you hear such language?"

"In the *Encyclopaedia Britannica*," I said, "it means . . ."

"Shut up!" said Derek. "Where is the kidney?"

"Mine?" I said, grinning. "It's about here, I think," and I poked my stomach.

"Did you or didn't you buy the kidney?" insisted Derek.

"I did!" I yelled. "But I'm not a pimp, I won't cater to your illicit appetites, your perverse habits, your lust! I simply won't! So I threw it away."

Slap!

Derek was pale and still. It would have been better to tell the lie about the boy.

"A boy stole it," I said sulkily, "and *he* threw it away and even the dog . . ."

What dog? the girl said.

"The dog. He wouldn't eat it either, so finally, a cat carried it away, you know how cats are, how they like nasty things." I happened to look at Derek's groin. "Derek!" I cried, at the delayed reaction to the slap. "Derek, don't hit me!"

"I apologize," said Derek coldly. "I'll dine at the club."

I didn't think he would but he did, at least he went out. He showered and dressed and reached into the closet for his Homburg and click! in my face the door closed.

"Don't leave your balls on the park bench!" I screamed in a fury.

If he had heard her, he would have killed her but the girl got the gun first. Click! In my face the door closed.

The girl, Sigourney looked at her in the mirror, her face was flushed, her eyes like wet stones, her hair hung over her eyes like tall grasses over the pond. Pretty, someone said. She favors Aunt Maisie. Allyn sat in the weeds and the skunk cabbages, setting the trap to catch the woodchuck. Out of his mouth came all the dirty words and little Sigourney put her fingers in her ears. But she heard the words or saw them, they were written down somewhere, but not in her prosaic little diary. She couldn't remember. Only when the time came to use them they came out of her

sulky mouth easily enough. It was Derek who made
her say them because she had never said them before. They had something to do with the honeymoon.
There's Honey on the Moon Tonight. Fuck you, said
Allyn.

No no no! the girl cried and hid her face, her
pretty shining face, in her hands, but the girl still
stood in the mirror and wouldn't go away. Bang!
You're dead, said Allyn, but the mirror didn't shatter.
I saw the girl walk backward to the reflected door
and I too went away backward, closing the door
gently so it wouldn't click. Besides, the gun was in
Derek's top drawer and the bracelet and the lipstick.
Now the girl would be gone out of the mirror because I closed the door, only the empty room is in the
mirror. "It's all make believe," I said out loud. It's all
make believe, isn't it Daddy? Yes, said Daddy, it's all
make believe, go to sleep. But what's the matter with
Mama? She's pretending, said Daddy. But I didn't
go to sleep because where was Derek? What was he
pretending to do? And was Marie pretending something, too? Was Derek pretending to be at the club
and was there a real club or was it a cutout? Whoever drew the picture didn't know anything about
perspective and everything is out of proportion, look
at the butcher's big red hand and his eyes too close
together, his apron a woman's skirt and flippers for

feet. It is a child's picture, crudely drawn with greasy
crayons, like the picture of Peter, his was white on
white, only the child could see it, Sigourney saw it,
she must have drawn it herself, but Peter at least was
in drawing while the butcher looked like a mutation,
maybe a fish, and in bright colors off key.

You're nothing but a girl, said Allyn, you haven't
got anything.

Shut up! yelled little Sigourney.

What do women know of love? said Derek.

Erase it, he didn't say it, not yet.

I couldn't sleep. It can't be true that Derek isn't
coming home at all. . . . But is it? Click! I seem to
hear the ominous sound of a door closing and then,
as if it were left ajar, a chill like a narrow draft, icy
like a knife. Something is final but what? What is
Louise laughing at and why is Blessèd crying? Her
face looks like a pillow after a pillow fight. Oh stop
it! Call Sydney.

"Sydney!"

No answer.

"Sydney! Come Sydney! You can sleep in here tonight. Sydney!"

How did you expect me to open the door? said
Sydney, stretching and grinning. I put on the light in
the kitchenette and glanced at the clock, it said 2:30.
Then I saw the little note on the table folded so
neatly, I reached out and lifted it up. I smelled it. I

didn't dare unfold it. Sydney went back into her bed under the table. I stood there. *Good-by forever*, the note said in Derek's fine aristocratic hand. But I still did not open it. *Your behavior is inexcusable*, it said, *your manners are frightful, your language is vile*. I was afraid to open it. *Marie is a very intelligent woman, Marie is ageless. Marie and I are going to Bermuda*. And what about *me*! I cried. I visualized our house in the country, dark, everyone asleep, the moon shone on the copper gutters outlining the eaves. The trunks of the big elms are black, their branches blurred like clouds overhead, charcoal clouds, with lightning in them, you can do it with a gum eraser, it's easy. I ran up the steps. I rang the bell but it never worked. Mama! Daddy! Delia! Sydney! What's the matter, what's the matter, what's the matter! I couldn't tell them, I was too ashamed, I just couldn't. The brute, said Daddy. The child's overwrought, said my grandmother. My grandmother is dead. A cup of tea, said Delia. Yes, I'll make myself a cup of tea, I put the silly little kettle on, the one I thought was so cute a week ago. Then I opened the note and read it: *Sigourney, please see if you can buy some truffles tomorrow. The tinned ones are very good. Derek.*

The rat!

I went into the living room and sat on the couch and thought for a long time, but not in words, like a silent movie, there wasn't even a commentator, I just sat in the front row and watched the man and the girl. It seemed a very touching picture to me and there were tears in my eyes. Yes it was a sad picture, what you call a tear-jerker. I was ashamed of my tears because it really was a corny movie: Good-by forever. Oh my love. It seems to be over. "Truffles," I said and stood up. I chose one of the books among the cookbooks on the lower shelf. I ran my finger down the index in the back: *Truffles*. What about truffles, anybody know anything about them, let's see, what is *their* evolution, get going. Here it is: *A truffle grows best on a pubescent (hairy) oak. It takes its nourishment from a sick root (Symbiosis)*. Ugh! I closed the book. First it's kidneys that look like you-know-what and now it's truffles sucking on the sick roots of a hairy oak. It's indecent and disgusting. A card slid out of the book: *Last night was simply divine. Merry Christmas, Marie;* and last year's date. That was the year I was supposed to come to my senses. There are lots of nice boys your own age, someone said, wait. That's just the trouble, the girl said flippantly. They come in lots.

Well, I finally went to bed; a sickly city dawn was drawn across my window like a piece of gauze, a veil over a face. "This is my honeymoon," I said bitterly, but the loony tune was gone, it didn't bother me, I went to sleep . . .

Nevertheless I heard voices, subdued but decipherable like branches that should have been cut back brushing against the windowpanes in an easterly wind. "Please," that was Peter, "for just a little longer," and Derek: "No, you can't come in, she might wake up." Silence, a long silence, or else half-asleep I can't remember, something was canceled. I heard nothing except finally the click of the door and my brain was too tired to make it sound like a gun that didn't go off.

But I am suddenly wide awake. I want to know something . . . What? Who is prompting me, is it the girl, my other self? Oh let me sleep! I can't. Mentally I take the little book out of the desk and thumb back the yellowed pages of my little-girl diary. On the last page is the word with a lot of exclamation marks: "Coconut! ! ! !" I feel a chill of fear at the notation I have seen before, but I cannot remember; some nastiness, some nastiness surely, because Allyn is nasty. There is no need to be afraid. I am exhausted and again I am almost asleep when it comes to me! Allyn had found his father's revolver in a bureau drawer. He shot the coconut through the head! That's what he said, through the head. I was terrified. I was a scaredy-cat. . . . So that's why I couldn't imagine the gun misfiring a minute ago . . . it didn't. But I don't remember the sound of Allyn's father's gun.

10

So Derek didn't go to the imaginary club at all. I woke up to find him still asleep in the other twin bed and I wasn't surprised because I must have known it in my sleep anyway and all my fears of desertion went away and Bermuda was nothing but one of a group of small islands east of Cape Hatteras, so I just felt stupid and I was glad Derek was asleep so I could look more intelligent when he woke up. It would only take a minute. I crept silently out of my virgin bed and I looked down on Derek. I had never seen him asleep before, I watched the girl looking at her unknown lover. I felt sorry for myself looking at the stranger. I recognized him, but that's about all. I had never really, perhaps had not dared, looked at him when he was alive. Intent on my own emotions, listening to my own heart, feeling the skip in my

pulse, the blood in my arteries, the smoothness of my
own skin, the depth of my eyes, the refraction in
them, I had never seen him before, I had just
watched the girl as I was now watching the girl
watching the man. Go away, I said to her. I stepped
in front of her. I looked over my shoulder and saw
her watching me in the mirror. She is so pretty. Why
is she unloved? Who is she? She is suffering from her
loss of identity, poor little thing. Tears came into my
eyes and I knew the girl in the mirror was weeping
silently and alone. With an effort I concentrated on
the man who lay there helpless under my eyes. He
might be dead. I didn't appreciate him when he was
alive and now he is dead. He is dead, I said as if I
had not heard myself, do you understand? Derek's
profile against the white satin pillow in the coffin was
very handsome, his one eyebrow arched over his
brow like a beautiful woman's, his one nostril flared
a little, a delicate susceptibility to something or
other, the perfume of the Chablis perhaps. His upper
lip is a little long and the lower one protrudes just a
little, almost a pout, like Peter's. I had never noticed
it before. His neck is long, he looks like a horse shy-
ing at a paper bag. I am a widow, I am grief-stricken,
I am too young to be left alone and unprotected.
"Derek, Derek, speak to me!"

"What's the matter?" said Derek.

"Oh Derek!" I cried, bursting into real tears. "I'm so sorry." But I wasn't, it was a leftover emotion that he had not given me time to fulfill, it was too bad. Now that he was alive, I wished him for that second dead, and now that he was alive I was on guard again, I had to be careful, I must hide the gun.

"Hand me my robe," said Derek. "I overslept."

"It's only me," I said, not moving. He was naked under the sheet. "I've seen you before," I said coolly.

Derek rose up out of bed like a brown genie out of a white bottle and strode across the room with as much dignity as if he were fully dressed. I giggled. "Whoops!" I said. As he passed the mirror, he had almost collided with the girl in it, his slim brown body eclipsed hers for a second. I know because I was watching. I felt a sudden thrill and raised my arms to clasp his neck, I saw the girl do it, I felt like a *voyeuse*. I pressed myself against him and in the mirror I saw his taut buttocks and his slim and elegant back and he being taller than the girl, I could only see her hands on the nape of his neck, but I heard her sigh although it was only a whisper of a sigh. I felt as weak as a kitten. It was delicious. With nothing on but my trousseau nightie and Derek as naked as a peeled willow switch, I felt myself a woman; my femininity came rushing back; all gone my childhood nastiness, Allyn, savage fertility sym-

bols and wordless images. My grandmother tore up
all the naughty drawings and flushed them down the
toilet. I even had the intuitive sense not to speak.
Aware of my body, I began to use it. The girl was
making love to the man; hidden behind him I
watched the hands that seemed disembodied, but
capable and so soft. The man would surely respond
to the new Sigourney, even though she was invisible.
Her breasts and belly caressed him and out of her
mouth came a long sigh and some shorter ones, a
moan like sugar.

But the man stood like a statue in the park. If he
stood there much longer, ivy would grow up his
smooth loins and oxidation whiten his greenish metal
locks. Besides, the Society for Decency had put a fig
leaf on him and the girl was wasting her femininity
on a thing cast *cire perdue*. How long would it take
the girl to realize that, dressed only in a transparent
nightie, she was attempting the statue of Nathan
Hale that stood at the entrance to the park, and for
all the world to see her failure, her shame.

Derek shuddered. Still warm from my sweet love I
drew away from him. His body had grown cold. I
shook my head to free my mind of the scene of the
girl bending over the coffin with the dead Derek in it.
I looked into his face as I drew back, my hands, such
pretty hands, like two birds, doves, still fluttering

around his neck and shoulders. I drew back to discover the cause of the shudder, of the cooling skin, the immobility, the fig leaf. What I saw was an unmistakable look of *disgust* and the contemptuous curl, like a shaving the carpenters leave, of his lower lip that in sleep had pouted so adorably. And the shudder that I still felt in my fingertips and had felt the length of my body was a shudder of horror. Why?

I was speechless. No dirty words came out of my mouth, no sarcasm, no clownish observation. Derek was suffering. Derek! That third party, the girl, left us, in a sense *I* disappeared because it isn't correct to say "*me* disappeared." Sigourney stared at Derek and watched in amazement as some unnamable horror took possession of him. Guilty as she always felt, forever in the wrong, awkward, unsophisticated, her breasts too small, her hips too narrow, this, this moment only, when she felt she had arrived, become a woman, ageless, Marie! surely she was innocent of any cruelty. She could not be the cause of the anonymous fear (yes Derek was afraid) that fitted onto his face like an awful rubber mask you can buy for a dime. He couldn't have seen the gun or heard the click when it misfired. It lasted less than a minute, the look of mingled disgust and horror and fear, because Sigourney turned away, she could not bear it, and reached out for the robe that lay over the chair with the roses on it and handed it to the naked Derek, and in that time that, womanly, she had given him, as if to fasten his fly, he rearranged his face. He became again the handsome really beautiful Derek and Sigourney still in the trousseau nightie, her face flushed, her hair in her eyes, felt like a simpleton, immodest and girlish, even pigeon-toed, nobody had given her time to fasten her fly!

And what do you think Derek said?

"Don't forget the truffles, will you?" Derek said.

"Shit!" said Sigourney as Derek disappeared into the dressing room and she was still saying it over and over when he came out in his pin-stripe business suit and his pointed shoes and the tie with the medallions on it.

"You won't, will you?" he said. He looked over the pretty schoolgirl, disheveled and sulky in the transparent atrocity that the stupid saleslady with the pancake make-up and blue eyeshadow had made her buy—"He'll love it," she said with a conniving grin. "You had better get dressed," he said, "you look a little . . ." He arched his brows and forced a smile.

"Disgusting?"

Derek shrugged and turned away and so she missed the look, whatever it was. Derek could shuffle his face like a pack of cards.

I didn't forget the truffles, neither did I try to dispose of them as I had the kidney in the trash can. Coming in a tin as they did, I felt no disgust bringing them home, although they did thump around a little. I even ate the silky dish of noodles *al dente* Derek prepared with the truffles sliced very thin on top.

"It's simply divine," said Marie. "You're a marvelous cook."

Oh yes, Marie is here for dinner, didn't you know! Do you think Derek asked me if I minded or did I want her or was it all right! I don't exist.

"Derek, now that Marie has gone let's have a serious talk."

Derek laughed. "What about, little Sigourney?"

"Is there a club and did you go to it last night?"

"No," said Derek calmly.

"Why not?" I said. "Why didn't you go to the club when you said you were going to?"

"I just said there wasn't any club," said Derek.

"Then why did you go to it?"

"I didn't."

I thought for awhile but nothing came of it, I was just making a fool of myself again.

"It's a manner of speaking," said Derek, just when I thought the conversation was over.

"Oh?"

"Like you going home to Mother."

"But I'm not."

"Exactly," said Derek.

"How can you and Marie stand eating those awful truffles?" I said, at a complete loss what to talk about seriously.

"You ate them."

"But I didn't *relish* them the way you and Marie did," I said, underlining *relish*. "To see you and Marie eating those things that take their nourishment from the sick root of a hairy oak seems perfectly perverted to me. Of course I'm just a fool," I added.

"What are you talking about?" said Derek.

"Sick roots and truffles sucking on them," I said, raising my voice, "that's what I'm talking about and kidneys! and Homburgs! you might as well eat . . . you might as well eat . . ."

"Go on," said Derek.

"Balls!" I shouted.

"Testicles are very good," said Derek.

"What!"

"In Texas," said Derek.

"Texas!"

"They're called calf-fries," said Derek patiently, "on the menu; they taste rather like scallops."

"Why don't you eat scallops then!" I cried. "Why must you eat something else that tastes like scallops

when there are perfectly good scallops!" I was un-
winding. Derek as usual had ruined the crisis. He always steals away my thunder.

"Homburgs?" said Derek.

"I don't know," I said.

"Were you suggesting I ate Homburgs?"

"No," I faltered, "just something that reminded
me of something else. Something else on a park
bench."

"Aren't you being a little perverse?" said Derek.
"Why not a perfectly good Homburg and leave it at
that?" He seemed very pleased with himself, almost
jaunty. "Any other business on the agenda?"

"Funny business," I said, "funny business on the
agenda."

"Now you're talking nonsense," said Derek. "Let's
go to bed."

"I don't want to," I said.

"Come along," he said, "I'll put you to bed."

"What was Peter doing here last night?" I said, re-
sisting the temptation to let the whole thing go.

"Who?"

"Peter," I said, "or something that reminds you of
Peter, something that looks like Peter and smells like
Peter and tastes like Peter but maybe is calf-fries!" I
was so pleased with myself I laughed. "Delicious!"

But I saw a dangerous spark in Derek's eyes. It
was time to retreat or advance. Which?

MAUDE HUTCHINS 159

"Peter!" I cried, it came to me. "*I* am Peter! It is *I* who remind you of Peter! *I* look like Peter, *I* smell like Peter, *I* taste like Peter. It is *I* who am your dish of testicles!"

Slap!

"Oh!" I cried. "You married me because I remind you of Peter! Look, my thatch of brown hair!" I shook it. "My beautiful deep brown eyes!" I opened them wide. "My mouth!" I pouted.

"I'll kill you!" said Derek.

"Give me the bracelet in the bureau drawer," I said, "and I will be an exact replica!"

"You little beast!" said Derek; he grabbed me.

"You're hurting me!"

He struck me again and again: Slap! Slap! Slap! He threw me down on the bed and straddled me. He bit my mouth and my neck and my shoulder, he tore off my pink dress and ripped off my bra, the hooks and eyes danced in the air. He's crazy, I thought.

"You're crazy!" I shouted.

He stood up, he was trembling all over. I couldn't help seeing, well, I'm not so ignorant and inexperienced as not to notice, it was right in front of me, I couldn't help seeing. He was mad with desire for me.

But I couldn't exactly appreciate the big moment I had been waiting for, my body stinging from the painful slaps, my mouth swollen with bites, and the fear of death in my heart. I looked down at my bare

breasts, my round belly, my swelling thighs as if I'd
never seen myself before.

Derek was looking, too.

"For Christ's sake, turn over," he said, "or cover
yourself up." The ecstasy or whatever the devil it was
was over. He pulled up the quilt. "I apologize," he
said.

"Think nothing of it," I said through my swollen
mouth.

He disappeared, and I did, too. There were no pictures in my mind. The girl was gone. I didn't bend
over myself and think, How sad, how pitiful. I
didn't imagine him dismembering me and stuffing
me in my trunk with the bright hinges on it that
Daddy bought me and was in storage because, I
waited for a long time, said Derek, and this is forever. But I might need it, I said. Whatever for,
where are you going dead or alive in your trunk with
the bright hinges? The Giants won, said the nice
boy. Before passing out, I tried desperately to remember what my choice insight had been, what it
was I had said to Derek that brought on the ecstatic
frenzy, but I am only hearing in my ears fragments
and phrases from the party: . . . It was a lovely concert. I adore Beethoven. Which one my dear? Bach.
Wrong side of the tracks. *Noblesse oblige.* Thanks
old man. Coricidin. She's a White Russian. I had to,

what else could I do? Idlewild. Here, use my lighter.
What possible difference does it make. You simply
stick it in the oven. Remind me to tell you . . .

"Drink this," said Derek.

But I had time to see the trunk that Daddy bought
me on the station platform, someone was pointing
at it. . . .

"Drink this," said Derek.

I just had time to see the blood beside the trunk on
the station platform. . . .

"Drink this," said Derek.

"No! No!"

"Calm down," said Derek, "it's just a glass of port."

I sat up, I felt fine, I was thirsty, I gulped down
the port and felt the blood circulating in my body. It
came up into my cheeks. You look very pretty, the
girl said.

"Somebody bit me," I said, feeling my mouth.

"I said I was sorry," said Derek. He handed me a
sweater. I put it on. Refreshed from the port and
subdued by his kindness, I opened my mouth to
speak. Don't tell him you're sorry, said the girl, why
should you be, he hit you, he's sorry, let him stay
sorry.

"The port was good," I said.

Derek looked as if he were about to speak but he
didn't, who was prompting him?

"I'm jealous!" I said suddenly before the girl could advise me. It was the one thing I knew better than to say.

Derek said nothing, he simply looked a little uneasy.

"Marie!" I said.

"Marie?"

Get out of it, said the girl.

"Marie is so beautiful," I said lamely.

"You're not jealous of Marie?"

"Oh heavens no," I said, "gosh no." Thank God, I said to myself, at least I know better than to show my feelings about another woman, especially a specific woman.

"I'm just jealous of all those other women," I said, "not Marie, gosh no."

"Oh," Derek laughed, he seemed quite amused.

"Like the married woman, when you were seventeen," I said, "with the plump hands, I saw her pull down the shade, you went up the steps and into her house and I saw her pull down the shade."

"Where were you?" said Derek, laughing again, "when I was seventeen?"

"Well, maybe you were a little older," I said, "but I was there, passing by in my perambulator."

Derek seemed to have had enough. . . .

"Shall we go to bed," he said.

"Yes," I said sweetly

"I think you'll be more comfortable if I sleep in the other bed tonight," he said.

"Oh yes, I'll be much more comfortable," I said. "It's so crowded," I added, "sleeping together."

"Goodnight," said Derek.

"Goodnight. . . . Derek?"

"Yes."

"The bracelet is so pretty."

"What bracelet?"

"Oh."

"Goodnight."

"Goodnight."

"What bracelet?" Derek had said just as I had said, remember? What bracelet! And then all of a sudden, it was all I could do not to sit straight up in bed. What lipstick!

"Are you asleep, Derek?"

No answer.

But I was too exhausted to get up and sneak a look into Derek's bureau drawer. What gun! I went to sleep.

11

Well, Derek is behaving like a handsome stranger. I am reminded of when I first met him and how politely he stared at me across the room at my cousins'. To think I am sleeping now with the stranger—at least in the same room. I have seen him naked. It is as if that first evening at my cousins' he had walked across the room naked. How awkward and cumbersome my cousins seemed with their red cheeks and their crew cuts and their collegiate mismatching coats and pants. There were other girls there, plump and flirtatious and slangy, cute. But he chose me, he walked across the room absolutely naked but so dignified, and after that everyone waited a whole year for me to come to my senses. It is as if it were beginning all over again. Am I to have a second chance? The naked stranger is still staring politely. What is he waiting for? You leave me alone and I'll leave you alone. Love? What do women know of love. My time is marked by the appearance and disappearance of the hateful Homburg. It is on the top shelf or it isn't on the top shelf, which means that Derek is here or he isn't here. When Sydney and I take a walk in the park I look for it on a park bench, once I thought I saw it . . .

It was swinging from Derek's long arm.

"What are you writing about?" said Derek.

I looked up, my pencil still on the line. "Top hat and tails," I said. That's a vulgar pun, said the girl. I quickly crossed out *tails* and wrote *tales*. I didn't understand exactly what kind of pun I had made, I was just being flippant because I didn't want to cry about something, I'm not sure what.

"Marie has asked us for dinner, she's a fabulous cook."

"Fabulosa, occupant," I said.

"What are you talking about now?"

"I'm speaking in tongues," I said. "If you don't understand, you don't understand, period!" I jabbed the period. "The honeymoon is over," I said, and pushed aside my pad.

"A story?" said Derek vaguely, he wasn't interested, he wasn't listening. This was the time, one of the times, I could have said, "I'm going to kill you," and he would say, "Did you enjoy the party?"

"Just pretending," I said. What was Mama pretending?

"Well, would you like to go?" said Derek.

"What shall I go *as*?" I said.

Derek disappeared into my closet and came out with the cocktail dress. He held it against himself, one long hand indenting the waist, one leg forward, the way they do in shops for you to get the effect. He raised his chin to see if I would buy it. With Madame's big enormous cultured pearls, said the saleslady.

"Oh Derek," I giggled, "it's so becoming! You wear it! And the bracelet . . ." I said, "and the lipstick." (What lipstick!) "I'll go as Peter," I improvised. Watch out! the girl said. I ducked, expecting the slap, but Derek turned and went back to the closet. He came out straight as an arrow but he was pale. The effort not to slap me had cost him some of his heart's blood. Forgetting to watch myself, watching him, I pitied him, a wave of pity, a new sensation, mounted me, stenciled my legs, caught in my throat. It was like a caress. Something new has been added, I thought. It is the man who is suffering. Possibly the man has been suffering all along but the girl had only eyes for her sister self. Why, I've scarcely needed

Derek for the sad story of me, he is a minor character, someone to provoke my responses, make me cry,
torment me. And now he is responsible for my feeling of pity, without him I wouldn't feel it.

Of course there was still time for him to slap me,
he didn't stand there as long as it takes me to write
all this, waiting for me to describe him, dress him in
his smart clothes, his pointed shoes, give him a meta-
phor: straight as an arrow, pale as . . . white on
white . . .

The tenseness, the pallor, is a substitute for hys-
teria perhaps, his way of not being hysterical rather;
and for the first time our parts are reversed. It is time
for *me* to change the subject. This is my cue.

"What shall we have for supper?" I said.

But I had unwittingly forced Derek out of his hole
like a fox, he looks like a fox, and like me he won't let
well enough alone. "What do women know of love!"
he cried, he flushed scarlet; it was disconcerting coming so quick after the extreme pallor, or did it take
longer? What was I thinking?

I tried again. "I would like so much to meet your
mother," I said. Who was feeding me the script? And
like me, Derek gave up, I couldn't be roused, and returned to himself. "I'll take Marie a bottle of Montrachet," he said. And then, "Mother isn't well."

I, too, back in character, said, "You are taking

Marie a bottle of Montrachet because your mother isn't well?"

"Didn't you say you would like to meet Mother?" he said.

"Did I?" I said, and if I did not reread what I had written I really forgot, because I was just playing Derek's part, I suppose.

"Why don't you run over this afternoon?" he said.

"Alone?"

"I'll call her and let her know you are coming. It's very nice of you, Sigourney. But don't tire her, she's not well." He kissed me on the cheek; you know, one of those absent-minded kisses as if you were going somewhere on the train for a week. The second he left, click, possibly because of the click, I had a fierce compulsion to look in his bureau drawer. I was excited, like a child left alone in the house that can't wait to explore the unknown, find the answer to secrets and discover forbidden fruit, bite into it, maybe steal Granny's peppermints, take a big gulp of Papa's Booths House of Lords, sniff at Mama's French perfume. It has something to do with sex. It's very exciting. But just as the child knows beforehand, as a dog has a prescience, really knows exactly where everything is and feels its persistent appeal, I knew what was in the bureau drawer: the bracelet, the lipstick . . . I reached further back and felt the coldness of

the gun. My heart beat very fast at this realization of
my insight, if that is what it was. Haven't I said again
and again, "What gun!" Haven't I heard the click
when it misfired? Or was it a door closing? I lifted
the gun out of the drawer and held it in the palm of
my hand. I stared at it. In spite of being a country
girl, I had never had a gun in my hand before that I
remember, so why did this one seem so familiar? I
wrapped my fist around the grip, my forefinger along
the barrel. I knew the revolver well. It fitted into my
hand as if made for me. . . .

The telephone rang.

I replaced the gun.

"Hello?"

"This is Peter."

"Which Peter?" I said, laughing.

"Tell Derek to answer the telephone."

"He isn't here"

"I've called before when I know he's there." Peter
sounded cross. I remembered the girl and the man
not answering the picture of the telephone.

"Stop calling him!" I said suddenly.

"What!"

"I said, stop calling him, he doesn't want to talk to
you."

I heard Peter laugh, a nasty little laugh. I was furious but I controlled myself, I said nothing.

"Tell Derek Louise got cut again."

"Tell Derek Louise got cut again," I repeated.

"Roger," said Peter.

"What do you mean?" I said, late as usual in my responses, I'm so moony.

"I mean she's all cut up but she'll get over it. She's tough."

"Who?" I said.

"Who do you think?" Peter said rudely. "Blessèd of course."

"Blessèd! I saw Blessèd on the john, her eyes drowned in tears—Weezie! Weezie!"

"Well, g'by, see you at Ma*ma's*." He hung up.

"Ma*ma's*," I mimicked. The sissy.

I walked and then took a bus uptown. I was going in the same direction, I could tell by the sun, as when I walked downtown at home, in fact, there wasn't any uptown at home. In the country it's always downtown, no matter where you start from. It's much nicer.

"Who shall I say is calling?" said the maid; no Delia she, she looked like one of the International Set in an apron.

"Sigourney Wagstaff."

So I waited in the hall. I can't describe the hall, it's as if I wasn't there, it might have been a box. I was thinking of Derek's terrible disgust—the more femi-

nine I get as I grow older, I am aging fast this year,
the more disgusted he is. And why should he suffer?
What right had he to suffer? The wave of pity did
not last long. What is the matter with him? I kicked
the rug.

"Sorry, miss, to keep you waiting, Madame was
resting. Come this way."

"The dear little bride!" someone said. Who? I
thought. Is there a little bride somewhere?

"I keep the room shaded," said Derek's mother. It
was practically pitch dark, so I shut my eyes, the way
you do in the theater, and opened them and I saw
Derek's mother and I guess she saw me because she
said, "How pretty you are. Come and kiss me, sweet
and twenty."

Shit, I thought, but it was nice. I liked her, she was
human. I had expected, well, something inhuman,
maybe a female computer.

"I'm an alcoholic," she said.

"I live in Connecticut," I said, "in the country, our
house was built in 1700. It's whittled on the beam in
the cellar." What else could I say? She had identified
herself, so I did, too.

"How quaint," said the old lady.

"Quaint?"

"Forgive me dear, it's from the past. A cellar! But
it's nice, a cellar, so cool."

For a second I had felt like an idiot but I laughed.

I could see the old lady by now, and she was an old lady, she wasn't ageless like Marie.

"You remind me of someone," she said, "your hair, your eyes . . ."

"Please!" I said.

"Psst, look dear," she said, "over there, behind the books, on the second shelf . . ."

I found the bottle. She quickly lifted it to her mouth. I was astounded, no glass, nothing.

"Here quick, child," she said, "put it back."

"Now," she said, "let's talk."

I said nothing.

"Don't be shy," she said. "Tell me, do you love my boy?"

"Oh yes," I said. "Oh," I said, "you mean Derek?"

"Naturally," she said; she had a pleasant laugh. I smiled at her.

"You're adorable," she said.

Alcoholic! I thought.

"Oh my child, save him, save him." She was weeping, all down the front of her dress, she was sopping wet, she dabbed at herself with some Kleenex.

I loved the dramatic appeal, my soul responded. But save him from what?

"I will," I said. "Oh I will," I promised with tears in my eyes.

She looked appealingly at the second shelf. I handed her the bottle.

"Have a snort?" She offered it to me.

"Oh no, thank you."

"I'll just take another quickie," she said, and tipped up the bottle again. She had stopped crying as suddenly as she began, her eyes were dry and bright. I hid the bottle again.

"What were we talking about?" she said.

I started to say "Derek," but I said, "I don't remember."

"He's all I ever had," she said. "Such a little man." Derek a little man! How funny! He was born standing up, impeccably dressed.

"Louise?" I suggested gently.

"Oh her," the old lady said. "I never liked her."

"Oh."

"Peter!" she said. "You're the image of Peter! The naughty boy."

"Would you like another snort?" I said.

"There's a dear," she said.

Maybe she will pass out, I thought, and I can go home.

"Marie," she said. "Have you met her?"

"Yes," I said guardedly.

"A very beautiful woman," she said. "May she drop dead."

"Madame," said the maid, "it's time for your Metrecal." She looked sharply at the old lady and then at me and back again, she peered around the darkened

room, and at her again. The old lady's face was
flushed, and she was happily rotating in her chair,
tapping her foot to some tune in her head.

"Madame!" said the maid accusingly.

"It isn't so," said the old lady. "I haven't had a
drop."

"I like your mother," I said to Derek. "She's real."

Derek seemed relieved. "She was all right?" he
asked, he looked at me sharply as the maid had
looked at his mother.

"Yes," I said, "she didn't have a drop." I felt a cer-
tain security in the old lady. We were conspirators, a
complicity between us.

"Darling," said Marie, kissing me on both cheeks,
"how smart you look!" How did she know? She was
looking over my shoulder at Derek. "Dear boy," she
said, and I remembered how he fell into step beside
her and how all the traffic went into slow motion,
even the delivery boy on a bicycle. He was such a
little man, said the old lady. I saw Derek straddling
his mother's lap. I hadn't been able to imagine it at
the old lady's, but here at Marie's I saw him plainly,
such a little man making love to his mother and she
was flushed, laughing, ageless, willing.

"Peter," said Marie, "you make the drinks, will

you sweetheart, I've something oh so good in the
oven, Derek. Duck Bordelaise. Yes, really. I mustn't
drink, it goes to my head." She looked at Derek and
laughed. What did they know between them? What
were they remembering? They disappeared in the
fog, Marie stretched and sighed as if she were in her
own room, Derek's long hand caressed her thigh. I
shook my head.

"You don't want a martini?" said Marie.

"Oh yes, I do," I said.

We sat around and everyone talked about food,
even Peter. . . . "You must flatten the squab very
gently with a mallet . . . exactly twelve minutes . . . a
tablespoon of cognac . . . detach the glaze carefully
. . . oh but duck Bordelaise . . . press the liver through
a sieve . . . veal Marengo . . . endive . . . shake the
casserole from time to time . . . Marsala is the best,
you beat it with a whisk. Peter, go baste the duck,
dear. . . ."

I stared at Peter. I remembered the exchange of
kisses long ago, the exchange of keys, what else had
we exchanged? How adorable he looks in that pink
shirt. "I want a pink shirt like Peter's," I said. No one
paid any attention.

". . . But you haven't tasted anything if you
haven't tasted . . . in Spain they . . . once in Madrid
. . . there's a little place on Third Avenue . . ."

"Have you ever had calf-fries!" I said loudly and sweetly to no one in particular and no one in particular answered. I looked at Peter, he was watching Derek. I looked at Marie, so was she. "I think I'll go home," I said. "I have a headache." No one heard me.

"What is your favorite dish?" someone said.

The bookshelves were full of books, not evenly arranged but lying against each other, some were stacked horizontally, they looked nice that way. There were flowers in a big china bowl. I'm over-dressed, I thought, Marie is in pants, smart ones, and jewels, an emerald bracelet . . . how beautiful she is!

"What is your specialty?" she said again, she was smiling at me, being a good hostess, trying to draw me into the conversation. I wasn't invisible then. I wasn't outside in the wind and rain peering in the window at the upper classes.

"Fricasseed chicken," I said.

"I imagine with a little Madeira, a white sauce with a little Madeira . . ."

"Vermouth, Ma*ma*," said Peter.

The conversation veered away from me again.

"Fricasseed chicken in disguise," I said, but my witticism went unheard, maybe I didn't say it. "Squeaky pork chops," I added. Derek is drinking more than usual, there is a stroke of color along his cheekbone like rouge. Marie has changed her mind and is sipping a Positano, Peter is stuffing himself with pâté.

"You shouldn't serve a pâté before dinner," said Derek. I looked at Marie. It was a criticism. But she kept on smiling.

"When then?" she said.

"Never," said Derek.

I longed to take a look at the books, there were nothing but cookbooks at our place. No one would notice. I recognized quite a few of the books I had read at home in the country, no one had ever stopped me. What she doesn't know she won't understand, said Mama. Balzac, *The Girl with the Golden Eyes; The Turn of the Screw* by Henry James; Nietzsche, *Thus Spake Zarathustra* . . . Stacks of wonderful new paperbacks, translations from the French, Italian and German. What a feast! I probably thought the word because I was starving; when in God's name would we eat!

"Look at the little bookworm," called Marie.

"She has very good taste," said Derek. I was pleased, I blushed. "Better than yours, Marie," he said. "You haven't any critical sense, you read a lot of trash."

"So do I!" I cried. I came to the defense of womanhood, "I love trash."

Marie remained imperturbable, but she poured herself another small glass of Positano.

"All women have lousy taste in literature," announced Peter. (Why, the little bitch! I thought.) I slid a book out of the shelf: Jean Genet. *Not to be sold in the U.S.A.* "What she doesn't know she won't understand," said Mama. . . . *terrible fairy vengeance* . . . I read.

"I asked the boys," I heard Marie saying, "to stop by after dinner . . ."

Then we *were* going to eat. I came back and reached for the remains of the pâté. I was so hungry. I picked out the truffles. I picked out the raisins in the pudding. They looked like swollen flies. "But they're the best part," cried Marie (said Mama). A tantalizing steamy perfume came out of the kitchen. You could almost see it like a vapor trail from a jet in the sky outside the little window, like two monkeys the jets spiraled after each other in the sky, like two monkeys up a palm tree. Bouk! a coconut fell on the ground and split open.

"My God the asparagus!" yelled Marie. "I forgot!" She ran for the kitchen.

"Not asparagus again," said Derek.

"It's all right," she said. They all sat and let the smells of sauces and flavorings tease them into a kind of ecstasy; Marie was smiling and languorous as if she were being caressed by an invisible hand.

The girl had ignored the No Trespassing sign and
had damaged the bed of tulips with her high heels as
she stepped through it in the dark. Her face appeared in the window. Not so much in the window as
on the window, pasted on the window.

"Draw the shades," someone said.

Yes ma'am, said Delia.

Marie was having another Positano from the fragile wine glass. Derek was drinking Scotch, straight, it
looked from the color, a big highball glass of it. He
began to talk. I listened amazed. His family had
taken him to the Continent (he said *Continent*)
when he was seven, they lived in France, he described Brittany. When he was fourteen, they en-
rolled him at Eton. He took his degree at Cambridge
although his father, who was English, preferred Ox-
ford. His mother was a Vanderbilt. She gave him
everything he wanted, she was a very beautiful
woman and had been presented at Court when she
was seventeen. Derek often, as a little boy, had tea
and scones with the Queen . . .

"Oh Derek, shut up," said Marie. "I'm fed up with
the story of your life." She turned to me. "It's nothing but a record you can't turn off," she said. "He
comes from Missouri, his family were poor, he never
had a cent to his name, he came East with only a
cardboard suitcase."

I couldn't imagine Derek with a cardboard suit-

case. I couldn't imagine a cardboard suitcase. I was
at a complete loss. Maybe I was in shock. Who are
these people? Peter was sulking. He, too, seemed
to have heard it all before. He was waiting. He sat
on the edge of a little gold chair, waiting. Then he
got up and went into the kitchen.

"Take a look at the duck," said Marie, "if it's ready,
and shake the casserole, don't take the top off."

I couldn't stand watching Derek, and Marie too,
disintegrating, falling to pieces like plaster of Paris
dolls. I followed Peter into the kitchen.

"Peter," I said, "oh Peter."

We looked into each other's own eyes and I longed
for him to kiss me in the mirror. I wanted to kiss the
pretty girl in the mirror, I wiped off the patch of
mist with a piece of Kleenex, suppose someone saw
me!

"I kissed you because I was mad at Derek," said
Peter. I didn't hear him, but he said it, I suppose.

"Kiss me," said Peter. My heart leapt. "I want
Derek to see us," he said.

"What! What Peter?"

He grabbed me.

"No, wait," I murmured as if it were real, it's what
I would have said, "No, wait."

Derek stood in the kitchen door.

I only had time to see the two bracelets on each

lean arm, each virile lean arm. I don't know yet if it
was a blow or an embrace.

I don't remember eating the perfectly marvelous
duck with the simply divine sauce or whatever had
been so gently shaken in the casserole, or the asparagus—"I'm tired of asparagus," said Derek.

"You really can't cook, Marie," said Derek. "The
sauce is god-awful . . ."

"Your emeralds are vulgar . . ."

"Women ought not to wear pants, your fanny
isn't what it should be, that blouse looks as if it came
from Bloomingdale's basement . . ."

Derek forgot his International Set accent, his pose,
his very posture, and reverted to common usage.

"At your age . . ."

Slap! Marie really swung on him!

"At your age," he repeated, "you ought to be baby-
sitting with your grandchildren, instead of . . ."

Marie hit him again hard and said some things I
can't bear to write down. . . .

Then: "Trick or treat!" The door flew open.

"Oh, you're just in time to wash the dishes!" cried
Marie. "Peter!" she called. "Bring in the coffee,
sweetheart."

It was as if I had imagined the awful scene, the
crumpled loss of Marie that I felt somehow more

than the metamorphosis of Derek. "Marie don't leave me!" I wanted to cry out.

It was the bums.

"It's the bums!" I announced, so astonished I did not think of how it sounded.

"Bums?" Marie looked at me, laughing.

"That's what Derek called them at the party," I said.

Marie laughed. "Oh my dear, he just meant they weren't his sort. They shouldn't have come to your party. Peter asked them to annoy Derek, they're just fairies, look at them, Carolinas right out of Genet!"

"Trick or treat!"

The bums were dressed in women's clothes with rouge on their cheeks and scarlet mouths.

"It's not Hallowe'en," I said stupidly.

"It's just an excuse," said Marie. "Oh you little monkeys!" She said it almost lovingly. "I'm surprised they let you up in the elevator."

"Baggage," they shrieked, "he's gay."

"Who?"

"The elevator boy, Fifi."

They were the same three bums that had enlivened the awful party in the little apartment: the one who had the look of a sailor, *Matelot, Matelot, When you go down to the sea;* the one who had very long lashes and dark holes in his cheeks as if he never

slept and when he looked in my direction once, he
looked as if he were facing a strong light, the pupils
of his eyes no bigger than a pin; the third was very
good-looking, almost as pretty as Peter, and it was
that one Peter chose to tease. "You little bitch!" he
had laughed when Peter bit his neck quick.

Dressed as girls, they were all startlingly pretty,
even if the make-up was a little smeary. The sailor
had chosen to wear pants, he must not have wanted
to hide the shape of his pretty buttocks, round as two
inverted cups, and a frilled low-necked blouse. Only
his Adam's apple gave away his sex and of course,
well, the pants were very tight. The one with the
amazingly long lashes (they came off later!) and
dark holes in his cheeks had covered his face and
neck with rosy pancake make-up and looked a little
more wholesome, but the blue eyeshadow and the
penciled lids only made his strange, almost pupil-
less gaze more disconcerting; the gold bangles from
the 5 & 10 did not cover up the punctures along the
insides of his bare forearms like pink freckles. He
frightened and fascinated me. I turned away from
him at once. But the handsome laughing one who
had called out "You little bitch!" at Peter and almost
set the stupid party spinning on its spike heels was
a darling. Her chestnut hair waved naturally from
the center over her forehead and cheeks, behind her

ears and low on her neck, caressing her round head
like soft fur on some little animal I can't think of
the name of, something that curls itself up on a bed
of leaves in a hollow tree, I saw a picture in a book,
but her eyes were soft and friendly, human, without
that fear for survival that the little curly animal had,
candid, innocent. She wore a white blouse open at
the neck and a short skirt. Only the legs were a little
muscular but perhaps she was a dancer. She was the
only one of the three who wore high heels, I could
hear her mother saying, You're too young, and her
reply, I'm seventeen.

"This is Sigourney, Derek's wife," sang out Marie.
They were all so pretty, I smiled at them with pleasure.

"How do you do," I said.

For a second they stood poised as if they might
attend to Marie's polite hostess-ship, as if they were
remembering the manners possibly taught them as
little boys by their mamas. I stood there just as pretty
as they in my cocktail dress and high heels, I only
lacked an Adam's apple. How could they tell what
was under my skirt, between my legs? The hesitant
indecisive manners only lasted that second as they
appraised me as I stood smiling. But almost immediately their pretty faces turned ugly. I was frightened. Would they take turns killing me! Would they

throw themselves upon me as the Nymphs did to
Orpheus and tear me to pieces, loathing my sex?

I stood my ground.

But they turned away, they had forgotten or
couldn't remember, it had only lasted a second.

"Alex!" called Peter. "Let's dance," and he took
the prettiest one in his arms. Alexandra, what a
pretty name!

That's when I noticed Derek and Marie had disappeared. Quickly they turned and walked away
into the pinkish fog and disappeared. Marie stretched
and sighed as if she were in her own room. Derek's
long brown hand caressed her thigh. Dear boy. The
door to Marie's bedroom was closed; the door to the
kitchen was wide open, no one was in there. The rain
beat down hard outside, and the bedroom door was
closed.

". . . Alex! Peter! Rudy! Sweetheart! Stop it! No!
No! . . ." The bums' voices were shrill, I hadn't noticed it at the party. . . . Marie and Derek were in
Marie's bedroom, Derek was caressing Marie, they
weren't quarreling any longer. Derek was elegant
again, lean and brown, and Marie was undressing.
Derek waited. He waited a long time because I
couldn't imagine Marie naked.

The door opened and they came out, Derek and
Marie, at least Derek came out, where was Marie?

Now Marie was carefully replacing her make-up, drawing on her lipstick, tidying her hair, putting on her high heels . . .

Derek!

An old man stood there, his body still lean and straight, straight as an arrow, lean as . . . but the face was ravaged by time. The inexpertly applied rouge made him look feverish and his cheeks drawn, the purplish eyeshadow, above and beneath the eyes, gave them a sunken desperate look, sick, lusterless. And the lipstick (What lipstick!) . . . ahhh, the lipstick made his mouth look like a crooked wound, a slash made by a knife! Blessèd slashed Louise across the face, Louise is a bitch, I hate her, Weezie! Weezie!

In spite of the passage of time that had made a horrible old man out of my beautiful Derek, everything else slowed down as it had done for Marie in the park, the boys' antics looked like slow motion. Marie, herself, who had been sitting over there all along, raised the glass of Positano to her lips so slowly that I wondered, I had plenty of time to wonder, if it would reach her lips before it evaporated completely. The dancing boys seemed to be dancing now a so-slow English waltz when the record was playing a samba and the machine played on and on and on and on . . .

"Derek come home!" No one heard me. "Derek

come home!" Oh save him! I will, I promise, but save
him from what?

Derek advanced into the room straight as an arrow, lean as . . . a wound in his aged face, his eyes
lusterless. The strange frightening boy caressed him,
but he was looking at Peter. Peter and the pretty
Alexandra were struggling on the couch, she
squealed and laughed, Peter was trying to undress
her but she was as strong as he—"No, no, you bad
thing!" Peter's hand was between her legs, her high
heels were scattered over the floor, seemed to be
still dancing. The sailor and the addict were twist-
ing. Marie stood, the fragile glass halfway between
her bosom and her lips, watching Derek. If it had
been Mama, she would have said, "I think it's time
your little friends went home," but Marie appears
to have lost track of everything. She is ageless.

Peter and Alexandra came to an understanding.

Derek gave a hideous scream. And then, "Peter,
come home!" he sobbed. I was the only one to hear
it but I didn't have time to think of the twin keys.
Quickly Marie swallowed the Positano, just in time,
because the little glass balanced on her lips only a
second before it fell to the floor, shattered, it broke
twice, once in the air and again as it struck the floor
. . . perhaps the piercing scream had broken it first.
The bums, Peter too, as if at a signal, someone had
blown a whistle, and Alexandra, turned on each

other, the crazy struggling felicity changed into a hysterical brawl but still body to body, mouth to mouth.

Slap! Slap! Slap! Who was slapping whom?

It became a melee, a silly riot. Slappity slap slap! Like clapping, it had a rhythm, it was keeping time to something, but no music. The record player had long since finished with the samba and the twist and the record itself was going round and round silently, some mechanism having gently lifted the needle out of the groove.

The furniture began cracking up, a little antique chair lay in pieces on the floor, its red velvet cushion still breathing like a scarlet lung. A kind of vicarious excitement, I suppose, made me want to stamp on the remains of the chair, really finish it off, but Marie was at my elbow steadying me.

"It always ends like this," she said. "The people below will be calling the police." There is a faint smile on her lips. "Perhaps you had better go home, dear."

Yes, surely, if it is a melee, a brawl, a disturbance of the peace, a riot, the police will arrive, summoned by indignant people below, and attracted by the rhythm will themselves join the dance, slap clap! slap clap! slappity clap! Clubs will swing around virile wrists. Peter will choose the handsomest, leanest, darkest officer and feel the muscles in his arms, his legs . . .

As if Marie was following my crazy illicit imaginings, she said, close to my ear, otherwise I couldn't have heard her, I think she said, "The law, the most devastating attraction of all: incest." I didn't get it, but Marie looked inspired, a strange smile on her face, that's the way she smiles for Derek. A very intelligent woman, said Derek. She reads a lot of trash, said Derek. I didn't get it. She will only understand what she knows already, Mama said.

My imaginings slowed down. Fags, said the police offstage, into the wagon with them. I heard the siren. But the sound of it, the wail of it, lasted longer than I meant it to, it got away from me, I couldn't stop it, it was on its own. I put my hands over my ears, Make it go away from Sigourney, I said. The child's overwrought, said my grandmother. A cup of tea, said Delia.

"I made you some fresh coffee," said Marie, "drink it."

"What happened?" I said.

"I guess you had one too many martinis," said Marie, "or something."

"Oh."

"And all the racket, and the music. I sent the boys home, little faggots," but she said it lovingly. Was it she who had said, Fags, into the wagon with them?

"Oh," I said again.

"Derek?" I said, suddenly sitting up.

"He's all right. Poor boy, he's so excitable."
(Derek! Excitable!) "He's in my room, resting."

Ahhh, she had comforted him. Why did my mind
keep harping on the disappearance of Derek and
Marie into the pink fog? Again I shook my head.

"You don't want the coffee?"

"Oh yes, I do. Thank you."

Immediately home from the brawl, scrubbed
clean, I am amazed at Derek's quick return to the
norm, his norm, and I feel released. There is no need
to save him from what. He is standing there in one
of his silences alone, I don't exist. He isn't naked but
I see him naked striding across the room at my
cousins' to choose me. I was given a year to come to
my senses. I love him. I too, quickly, within the hour
have come back to myself, to my norm. The brawl
at Marie's that I had seen through the window, standing in the tulip bed, will take a long time to become
a memory and clarify itself in my mind. I am living
in the present. You live in the present, Derek said.

"Derek?"

"Yes," said Derek but he meant *no,* in a minute
he would say something anticlimactic. Here we go
again.

"It's my honeymoon!" I wailed (Why must I play
the same scene over and over?).

"What honeymoon?" said Derek.

(What bracelet!)

(What lipstick!)

(What gun!)

The girl raised the revolver, it fit into her hand as
if it were made for her; the gun seemed colder and
heavier, her slim finger along the barrel trembled
as she pointed at Derek; sighting carefully, the tiny
piece of metal on the end of the gun looked like a
helpless sparrow on a branch, coolly, yes she was
strangely calm, she crooked her forefinger, she had
time to think how appealing and feminine the gesture was. Bang you're dead, she said.

The gun exploded.

But there was a lag in the timing. Derek had
gently closed the door behind him.

The sound was not very loud, one had to be listening for it to hear it and Sigourney was. Sigourney
was listening. It sounded just like when Allyn fired
his father's revolver into the coconut. Turn your
back, I'm going to shoot myself in the head, said
Allyn.

The gun didn't misfire.

The girl opened the door. Look, said Allyn, at the
brains and stuff, he made her look and to the frightened girl the milk was scarlet.